SIR GAWAIN AND THE GREEN KNIGHT

Sir Gawain and the Green Knight was written in the late fourteenth century by an unidentified poet from the Cheshire area, who was familiar with the rituals of aristocratic life and with French romance. The work is preserved in a single manuscript together with three other poems—*Pearl*, *Patience* and *Cleanness*—generally taken to have been written by the same author, and which further demonstrate a familiarity with clerical Latin learning.

KEITH HARRISON is an Australian-born poet and translator who has published widely in England, America and Australia. His numerous books of verse include *Points in a Journey*, *The Basho Poems* and *A Burning of Applewood (New & Selected Poems, 1958–1988)*. He has won awards for his work from the British Arts Council and the Bush Foundation. Currently Emeritus Professor of English at Carleton College, Northfield, Minnesota, he is presently working on his *New and Collected Poems* (1958–1988).

HELEN COOPER is Professor of English Language and Literature in the University of Oxford, and Tutorial Fellow, University College, Oxford. She is the author of *Oxford Guides to Chaucer: The Canterbury Tales* (Clarendon Press), and editor of Malory's *Le Morte Darthur* for Oxford World's Classics.

OXFORD WORLD'S CLASSICS

*For almost 100 years Oxford World's Classics have brought
readers closer to the world's great literature. Now with over 700
titles—from the 4,000-year-old myths of Mesopotamia to the
twentieth century's greatest novels—the series makes available
lesser-known as well as celebrated writing.*

*The pocket-sized hardbacks of the early years contained
introductions by Virginia Woolf, T. S. Eliot, Graham Greene,
and other literary figures which enriched the experience of reading.
Today the series is recognized for its fine scholarship and
reliability in texts that span world literature, drama and poetry,
religion, philosophy and politics. Each edition includes perceptive
commentary and essential background information to meet the
changing needs of readers.*

OXFORD WORLD'S CLASSICS

Sir Gawain and the Green Knight

A Verse Translation by
KEITH HARRISON

With an Introduction and Notes by
HELEN COOPER

OXFORD
UNIVERSITY PRESS

OXFORD
UNIVERSITY PRESS

Great Clarendon Street, Oxford OX2 6DP

Oxford University Press is a department of the University of Oxford.
It furthers the University's objective of excellence in research, scholarship,
and education by publishing worldwide in

Oxford New York

Athens Auckland Bangkok Bogotá Buenos Aires Calcutta
Cape Town Chennai Dar es Salaam Delhi Florence Hong Kong Istanbul
Karachi Kuala Lumpur Madrid Melbourne Mexico City Mumbai
Nairobi Paris São Paulo Singapore Taipei Tokyo Toronto Warsaw

with associated companies in Berlin Ibadan

Oxford is a registered trade mark of Oxford University Press
in the UK and in certain other countries

Published in the United States
by Oxford University Press Inc., New York

Translation first published by the Folio Society 1983
First published as an Oxford World's Classics paperback 1998

British Library Cataloguing in Publication Data

Data available

Library of Congress Cataloging in Publication Data
Gawain and the Green Knight.
Sir Gawain and the Green Knight : a verse translation / by Keith
Harrison ; with an introduction and notes by Helen Cooper.
(Oxford world's classics)
Includes bibliographical references.
1. Gawain (Legendary character)—Romances. 2. Knights and
knighthood—Poetry. 3. Arthurian romances. I. Harrison, Keith.
II. Cooper, Helen, 1947– . III. Title. IV. Series: Oxford
world's classics (Oxford Univeristy Press)
PR2065.G3A34 1998 821'.1—dc21 98–15783

ISBN 0–19–283334–0

3 5 7 9 10 8 6 4 2

Typeset at the Spartan Press Ltd.
Printed in Great Britain by
Cox & Wyman Ltd.
Reading, Berkshire

CONTENTS

ACKNOWLEDGEMENTS

An enterprise such as this depends on a community, and I have been particularly fortunate in mine. It stretches from the centre of America, west across the Pacific to Australia, and east over the Atlantic to England. From the outset, President Robert Edwards, Dean Peter Stanley, and the Trustees of Carleton College gave me considerable encouragement in my early work on the poem. I am also grateful to the Bush Foundation for a Fellowship in Literature that allowed me to make my first experiments in translating this work. Beyond that, the complete list is too long to specify, but I wish to give particular thanks to the following: my friends and colleagues of the English Department at Carleton College; Professors George Russell of the University of Melbourne, James May of St Olaf College, Linda Clader and Jackson Bryce of Carleton College—all for their warm and continuing support. For the preparation of various versions of the text I am most grateful to Barbara Jenkins and Carolyn Soule. Their patience has been astonishing, as has that of Carl Henry, Les La Croix, Marilyn Hollinger, Mark Heiman, and the entire staff of the Computer Center at Carleton College.

A number of other people have been so generous that I cannot adequately acknowledge my debt to them: Jennifer Strauss and Philip Martin of Monash University, Melbourne; Rodney Shewan, Davis Taylor, and Heather Dubrow of Carleton College; and the late A. K. Ramanujan, poet, translator, and friend 'in trawthe'—who read the manuscript with great care and made numerous suggestions without which this version would have been much the poorer. Kevin Crossley-Holland has made this enterprise possible in more ways than one. He has been a constant inspiration as a friend and as a superb translator from the Old and Middle English; trying to measure up to his standards has been the best, and the most rigorous education a translator could undergo. Finally, Professor Helen Cooper of University College, Oxford, has offered many excellent suggestions which have made me listen to the language of the original with renewed concentration and allowed me to correct some egregious errors. My warmest thanks to all these friends, colleagues, and teachers whose care and astuteness have helped make my work so rewarding.

KEITH HARRISON

Northfield, Minnesota
Fall 1997

INTRODUCTION

Sir Gawain and the Green Knight is one of the best Arthurian stories ever told, and one of the supreme achievements of medieval English poetry. It tells of how, one New Year's Day at the court of King Arthur, a huge green stranger disrupts the feast to offer a bizarre challenge—a challenge which only the king's nephew, Sir Gawain, has the courage to take up. The skilful characterization offered by the story is paralleled in the Middle Ages only by Chaucer; for its subtlety of narrative organization, one has to look much further ahead, to the eighteenth or nineteenth century, to find anything comparable. Despite its unnerving plot, it has often been compared to a novel for the sense it gives of a real character coping with a real world, and to film for its brilliant use of perspective and point of view. The language of a novel, however, could never match the powerful rhythms and muscular texture of its alliterative verse, which the smoother patterns of modern English cannot reproduce in prose and only with difficulty in poetry. A good translation needs to convey that sinew and energy of the poem's language and versification, even though they might seem to be inseparable from its archaic form. Keith Harrison's account of his work on the poem in the Translator's Note, pp. xxxix–xlii, gives some idea of how he has set about the challenge of conveying the power, as well as the sense, of the original.

The poet

Nothing is known of the *Gawain*-poet other than what can be deduced from the poem itself, and the single manuscript in which it is preserved—now London, British Library MS Cotton Nero A. x. (The name comes from the seventeenth-century antiquarian and collector Sir Robert Cotton; from the bust of the Roman emperor on top of the particular bookcase in which he housed it; and its place on a specific shelf.) The manuscript contains three other poems, all religious in subject: *Pearl*, *Patience*, and the poem named by different editors as *Purity* or *Cleanness* (the poems are unheaded, so all the titles are editorial). *Patience* and *Cleanness* are written in long-line alliterative verse, like *Gawain* itself, though without the rhyming 'bob and wheel' that divides that poem into stanzas. *Pearl* is written in intricately rhyming twelve-line stanzas, with abundant alliteration within the lines as well. All four poems belong to the same period, the later fourteenth century, and the same dialect area, which has been located to the border of south-east Cheshire and north-west Staffordshire: the precise detail of this location may however represent the origin of the scribe who copied the poems into the manuscript rather than of the poet himself, who certainly came from the same region but may not be possible to locate with quite the same degree of exactness.[1]

The precise date of the poems is also hard to pin down. It is generally agreed that the manuscript was copied no later than 1400, and that the poems were composed some time before that—conceivably as early as 1350, though the 1370s or 1380s would seem more likely from the details they give of the latest fashions in clothing and architecture.[2] The end of the century, when Richard II gathered a large body of Cheshiremen around

[1] H. N. Duggan, 'Meter, Stanza, Vocabulary, Dialect', in *A Companion to the Gawain-Poet* edited by Derek Brewer and Jonathan Gibson (Cambridge, 1997), 240–2. This volume (hereafter Brewer and Gibson) is a very useful summary of past scholarship on the four poems of the manuscript as well as taking research forward. The dialect locality was first established by Angus McIntosh, and confirmed in *A Linguistic Atlas of Late Mediaeval English*, ed. McIntosh, M. L. Samuels, and Michael Benskin (Aberdeen, 1986), iii. 37–8.

[2] The possibility of an early date for the poems is argued by W. G. Cooke, 'Sir Gawain and the Green Knight: A Restored Dating', *Medium Ævum*, 58 (1989), 34–48. The rather clumsy illustrations found in the manuscript were added after the writing was completed: Kathleen Scott, *A Survey of Manuscripts Illuminated in the British Isles VI: Later Gothic Manuscripts 1390–1490* (London, 1996), ii. 66–8.

himself at court, has also been suggested as a possible context for
the poet's mixture of courtly sophistication and provincial
dialect. The order of composition for the four poems is also
entirely conjectural. A fifth northern poem preserved in a different manuscript, *St Erkenwald*, a legend of the founding of St
Paul's, has been tentatively ascribed to the same author, but the
evidence is inconclusive.[3]

Despite their differences in poetic medium and subject, the
four poems of the Cotton manuscript show marked similarities
of method and preoccupations as well as dialect. If they are
indeed the work of a single poet, then more extensive deductions
about his identity become possible than if he wrote *Sir Gawain*
alone. He was, for a start, male: that is shown by the familiarity
with the Latin Bible and other homiletic works demonstrated in
the three religious poems, Latin learning being effectively a male
prerogative in the Middle Ages. Medieval education was also
largely inseparable from the Church, so the same range of
learning suggests that he may have been a cleric in minor
orders.[4] That he was not an ordained priest, or the holder of any
Church office that entailed either the duty of preaching or the
practice of celibacy, would seem to be indicated by various
passages in the poems that claim to be first-person experience. In
Patience he describes himself as being on the receiving end of
sermons, rather than preaching them. In a remarkable passage
hard to parallel in medieval ecclesiastical writings, he makes God
speak in feeling defence of the delights of sexual activities in
Cleanness;[5] and in *Pearl* the dreamer-narrator describes himself
as grieving for the death of a baby girl who died at less than two

---

[3] The London subject of the poem would fit with the *Gawain*-poet's possible
associations with the king's Cheshiremen, though the dates are at the latest edge of
possibility.

[4] On the extent of the poet's Latin learning, see Richard Newhauser, 'Scriptural and
Devotional Sources', Brewer and Gibson, 257–75; on the nature of his contribution to
vernacular theology, see Nicholas Watson, 'The *Gawain*-Poet as a Vernacular Theolog-
ian', Brewer and Gibson, 293–313.

[5] *Cleanness*, 697–708 (see Select Bibliography for editions).

years old. It may be that none of these passages is written out of autobiographical experience (*Pearl* could, for instance, be written for a patron in such a situation, or as more general advice to bereaved parents), and indeed the relationship of the girl in the dream to the dreamer is specified only as being 'nearer than aunt or niece'; but most first-person narrators of medieval poetry bear at least some relation to the poets who create them, and there is no compelling reason to doubt in this case why the poem should not have been occasioned by the death of the poet's own daughter. There are various hypothetical biographies one could construct for the poet to explain this apparent mixture of clerical learning and lay experience. He could have received an education as the younger son of a gentry family, perhaps destined for the Church but never taking orders. Alternatively, education would be a way of opening up the worlds of the Church, administration, and diplomacy to the son of an aspiring middle-class family; it could serve as the preliminary to becoming a clerk or secretary in a gentry or magnate household, or to obtaining one of the many household offices —steward, chamberlain, marshal—for which a clerical education was by no means necessary or customary, but might none the less be useful.

In addition, the poet was well versed in courtly French literature. He knew the great French allegory of love, *The Romance of the Rose*; and *Sir Gawain* itself shows his familiarity with French Arthurian romance.[6] He need not have acquired this knowledge in France, though the military and administrative activities of the English (not least Cheshiremen) in France in the middle stages of the Hundred Years War, or mercantile connections between the countries, could easily have given him such an opportunity. Manuscripts of French works of this kind were available in some numbers in England, French being gradually displaced as the language of the court and of administration only towards the end of the fourteenth century, and remaining as the

[6] See Ad Putter, *Sir Gawain and the Green Knight and French Arthurian Romance* (Oxford, 1995).

language of international culture and commerce for much longer.

As this familiarity with Latin and French attests, the *Gawain*-poet was by no means a provincial or dialect poet in any parochial sense. His home region—Cheshire and its borders with the surrounding counties, Staffordshire, Derbyshire, and south Lancashire—had a thriving cultural and political life in the late fourteenth century, and the *Gawain*-poet was not the only poet active in the area.[7] At this period the earldom of Chester was held by the Crown, and Richard II, who acceded to the throne in 1377, made increasing use of the connection. The second great barony of the region, the duchy of Lancaster, was held by his uncle John of Gaunt, third son of Edward III and the most powerful man of the kingdom after Richard himself. This meant that there were no great magnates resident in the area, but that relations with the royal court were close; especially so in the late 1390s, when Richard II retained several hundred men from Cheshire—many of them yeoman archers, but some seventy knights and squires as well—to serve as his personal bodyguard. The numerous gentry families of the region not only ran local affairs but carried an increasing influence in the Church and state: they performed military service in France, and reached high office in every field open to them. The lives of two men from the region contemporary with the *Gawain*-poet—one almost certainly younger, the other perhaps slightly older—will indicate how far ambition and ability could reach; both biographies are suggestive for the poet, though in different ways. The first, of the ecclesiastic Robert Hallum, might under different circumstances have been the poet's own; the second, of a rising member of the gentry, Sir John Stanley, indicates the kind of reader for whom the poem might have been written.

Robert Hallum, born around 1360 in Warrington in southern

---

[7] See Michael J. Bennett, *Community, Class and Careerism: Cheshire and Lancashire Society in the Age of Sir Gawain and the Green Knight* (Cambridge, 1983); and, on the regionalism of the Alliterative Revival, p. xxxiv below.

Lancashire, exemplifies a cosmopolitan career founded on learning. He made his way up within the academic world to become, in 1403, Chancellor of the University of Oxford; but that was no more than a step in his career in the ecclesiastical hierarchy, partly pursued at the papal court. He was indeed nominated by the Pope as Archbishop of York, but the appointment was vetoed by Henry IV; he was created Bishop of Salisbury instead, and brought numerous Cheshire clerks south with him to staff his household. In 1415, as one of the English ambassadors to the great Church council of Constance, he and a fellow English bishop urged an Italian cleric to make the first translation of Dante's *Divine Comedy* into Latin, the international language of learning. The completed translation, with a basic commentary for those unfamiliar with Italian history, was dedicated to the two bishops.[8] It has been suggested on occasion that the *Gawain*-poet knew the *Comedy*; Chaucer certainly came to know the work in the course of his visits to Italy, but otherwise there is negligible evidence for its being known outside its own language area in the century after its composition. Even though the translation was made too late for the *Gawain*-poet to have read it in this form, it is none the less interesting that one of his compatriots could reach such a keen appreciation of Dante's masterwork through a career that started from the same basis as the poet's, in scriptural learning.

The second biography is that of Sir John Stanley, an administrator and man of action who has some curious incidental connections with poetry and legend. The second son of Sir William Stanley of Storeton, in Cheshire, he was born around 1340, and, like many Cheshiremen, saw military service in France. One of his first entries into historical record is his receipt of a royal

[8] Bennett, *Community, Class*, 155–60; A. B. Emden, *A Biographical Register of the University of Oxford to AD 1500* (Oxford, 1957), ii. 854–5. Giovanni Bertoldi de Serravalle's translation of the *Divine Comedy* has been edited by M. da Civezza, MO, and T. Domenichelli, MO, as *Johannes de Serravalle: Translatio et Comentum totius libri Dantis Aldigherii* (Prato, 1891).

pardon for killing his cousin; the circumstances are unknown, but they evidently did not hinder his rise in the king's employment, since he served as deputy governor in Ireland and in various offices in Chester and the North-West. He was appointed surveyor and master forester of three of the great forests of Cheshire, in more or less the areas in which Bertilak in the poem goes hunting, by Henry IV, who also made him a knight of the Garter and steward of the royal household. He was the kind of man who became the subject of legend: by the sixteenth century, family tradition asserted that he had had an affair with the daughter of the Grand Turk, and left her pregnant. Better documented is the story of his death: returning to Ireland in 1413, he alienated one of the Irish bards sufficiently for a deadly lampoon to be composed against him, 'and he lived only five weeks till he died from the venom of the lampoons'. He had speeded his upward social trajectory by marrying the heiress of Sir Thomas Lathom, who was himself the subject of legend—in his case, that he had originated as a foundling rescued from an eagle's nest: the story gave rise to the badge carried later by the Stanleys, of an eagle with a swaddled baby.[9] At the end of the fifteenth century, their descendants, by this time earls of Derby, were themselves the focus of a series of poems celebrating, or where necessary inventing, their military exploits.[10]

Poetry was rarely written in the Middle Ages primarily for self-expression. Most often, as with other art forms, it would be produced for a known and appreciative reception group, or for a

---

[9] On Stanley's career, see Barry Coward, *The Stanleys: Lords Stanley and Earls of Derby 1385–1672: The Origins, Wealth and Power of a Landowning Family* (Manchester, 1983), 3–4, and *Victoria County History: Chester* (Oxford, 1979), ii. 167. On the legends, see 'The Stanley Poem' of *c.* 1562, ed. James Orchard Halliwell in *The Palatine Anthology* (London, 1850), 208–71 (on the Grand Turk, 211–13; on the foundling in the nest, 217–18, and Christa Grössinger, *The World Upside-Down: English Misericords* (London, 1997), 75 and pl. 113). For his death, see Gearóid Mac Eoin, 'Poet and Prince in Medieval Ireland', in *The Court and Cultural Diversity*, ed. Evelyn Mullally and John Thompson (Cambridge, 1997), 3–16 (quotation from p. 14).

[10] See David Lawton, '*Scottish Field*: Alliterative Verse and Stanley Encomium in the Percy Folio', *Leeds Studies in English*, NS 10 (1978), 42–57.

patron; and Sir John Stanley has increasingly been canvassed as a possible candidate for such a role.[11] The manuscript in which *Gawain* survives, unusually for a collection of English poetry, is illustrated, and was clearly made with some pretensions to being an elegant volume for an owner of at least the gentry class (though it has to be acknowledged that the pictures do not contribute to the elegance other than by the fact of their existence; compared with most manuscript illustration, they are singularly clumsy). *Sir Gawain* itself, moreover, appears to have been written for a knight of the Garter, the order of chivalry instituted by Edward III in 1348, since the poem concludes with the founding of just such an order, and the motto of the Garter knights is inscribed at the end of the poem. At first glance, Stanley is just the kind of person, with interests both at court and in the North-West, to match the mixture of regional English and courtly sophistication of the poem; and Storeton and Lathom are in the corner of Cheshire that forms the last identifiable location in Gawain's journey to meet his fate. The events in Stanley's career that might make him seem most appropriate as a patron, however, occurred after the composition of the poems: the forestships in 1403; incorporation into the Order of the Garter in 1405; the explicit connections with poetry, with himself as its victim or his descendants as the subjects of panegyric, even further distanced from the *Gawain*-poet. None the less, he may serve as an example of the kind of patron for whom the poet might have been writing, even if he were not the man in question; just as Hallum could serve as an example of what the *Gawain*-poet's own career might have been like, if he had had more ambition, or more ecclesiastical

---

[11] The idea was first propounded by Gervase Mathew, *The Court of Richard II* (London, 1968), 166; for a recent discussion, see Ad Putter, *An Introduction to the Gawain-Poet* (London and New York, 1996), 34–6. E. P. Wilson suggests a broader Stanley connection in '*Sir Gawain and the Green Knight* and the Stanley family of Stanley, Storeton and Hooton', *Review of English Studies*, NS 30 (1979), 308–16, in which he also notes that the family owned some manuscript poetry in the mid-15th century.

patronage, or even perhaps decided that the way of celibacy was not for him.

The romance background

The contexts out of which *Sir Gawain and the Green Knight* emerges are of two kinds: the broad cultural conditions and ideas that are reflected in the text, and specific works that may have provided the poet with plot motifs and the conventions that he borrows, alters, and exploits. Most Middle English romances were adapted from originals in the leading languages of romance, French and Anglo–Norman—that is, French as spoken either on the Continent, or in England in the centuries after the Norman Conquest. Some of the greatest 'French' romance writers of the Middle Ages, probably including Marie de France and the Thomas who wrote *Tristan*, were English in this geographical sense; it is misleading to think of the romances produced in England as always the poor neighbours of their Continental counterparts. The *Gawain*-poet belonged to an age when Anglo-Norman romance had ceased to be written, but being English no more consigns him to a cultural backwater than does being from Cheshire.

The immediate antecedents of many of the plot elements of *Sir Gawain and the Green Knight* lie in French Arthurian romances, though it is unusual in not having any one single source. There is no source at all for the most distinctive of its story motifs, the knight who is green not only in clothing but in skin and hair as well. Its principal plot motif, by contrast, the invitation to behead a challenger in exchange for being beheaded later, appears in a number of texts, and can be traced as far back as Irish legend. The version closest to that of *Sir Gawain*, and almost certainly known to the poet, appears in the *Livre de Caradoc*, part of the 'First Continuation' of the *Conte del Graal*, otherwise known as *Perceval*, which the late twelfth-century writer Chrétien de Troyes had left uncompleted (thereby offering an irresistible invitation to later authors to provide continuations). Here, the challenger appears at Arthur's court at the feast of Pentecost; Carados himself takes up the challenge, and beheads him. This knight puts his head back on before he speaks—in contrast to one of the most gruesome moments of *Sir Gawain*, in which the decapitated head speaks while the Green Knight holds it in his hand. A year later, he returns to the court and demands his return blow; after twice merely feinting at Carados with his sword, he finally strikes him with the flat of the blade, and then reveals himself as his father.[12] The story thus tells of a crucial moment in Carados's progress into full manhood—a rite of passage to chivalric maturity, such as *Sir Gawain* also recounts. By contrast, when the beheading motif reappears in another English romance of Gawain, *The Carl of Carlisle*, recorded in the seventeenth century but possibly originating around the same time as *Gawain and the Green Knight*, Gawain's beheading of the monstrous carl releases him from enchantment and turns him back into a normal human knight.[13]

The transference of another knight's French adventures onto an English Gawain is an indicator of Gawain's centrality in the English Arthurian tradition. He had initially emerged as a major character in Arthurian history in Geoffrey of Monmouth's twelfth-century *History of the Kings of Britain*, in which he is Arthur's right-hand warrior in his campaigns of European conquest. He appears frequently in the verse romances of Chrétien de Troyes, from the end of the century, but only in supporting roles: his function is to serve as a foil to the heroes of the various romances, by their proving their prowess in combat against him,

[12] For a translation of the relevant section, see Elisabeth Brewer, *Sir Gawain and the Green Knight: Sources and Analogues* (Cambridge, 1992), 25–32; the whole eposide, which forms a small romance in its own right, is translated by Ross G. Arthur, *Three Arthurian Romances: Poems from Medieval France* (London, 1996).

[13] In *Sir Gawain: Eleven Romances and Tales*, ed. Thomas Hahn (Kalamazoo, Mich., 1995), 373–91. A medieval version, *Sir Gawain and the Carl of Carlisle* (pp. 81–112), tells a closely similar story but without the release from enchantment.

or, in the *Conte del Graal*, by serving as a type of secular chivalry in contrast to the hero Perceval's more religious model. In another of Chrétien's romances, he is displaced altogether by the knight who was to become Arthur's closest associate in the French tradition, Lancelot. It is Lancelot who is the central character after Arthur himself (or even in preference to Arthur) in the great Vulgate cycle of French prose romances, of the thirteenth century, where Gawain slips even further down the ethical and chivalric scale, to the point where he often functions as an antitype of good knighthood. Morgan le Fay, the most enigmatic character of *Sir Gawain*, has a comparable history: invented by Geoffrey of Monmouth for his *Vita Merlini*, where she is a shape-shifter skilled in the arts of healing, she is given her place in the Arthurian orbit by Chrétien, who makes her Arthur's sister (and so also sister to Gawain's own mother—both are later re-defined as Arthur's half-sisters, born to his mother by her first husband); the prose romances degrade her into an evil enchantress, with a particular hatred of Guinevere. Unlike Gawain, however, who is the dominant character in the English tradition, Morgan plays little part in English Arthurian romance before Sir Thomas Malory's adaptation of various of the Vulgate cycle romances in the late fifteenth century. The *Gawain*-poet is the only writer to offer a close plot connection between the two characters, though it defies the best efforts of readers to define just what that connection is.

The *Conte del Graal* and its continuations were also instrumental in casting Gawain as a womanizer, and the characterization is taken further in other French romances. Tempted by a beautiful woman with whom he has to pass the night in a perilous bed, Lancelot will show his high chivalry by turning his back on her; Gawain will show prowess of a different kind by pursuing consummation through an unremitting onslaught of magic swords and flaming arrows. The English Gawain is placed on occasion in overtly sexual situations—in the *Carl of Carlisle*, for instance, his host orders him into bed beside his naked wife, but then forbids him to do more than kiss her, and rewards him with his daughter for a night of love followed up by marriage; but Gawain never appears as a lecherous figure until some time after the writing of *Sir Gawain and the Green Knight*, most notably in the French-derived sections of *Le Morte Darthur*.[14] In England, Gawain remains what he had been in Geoffrey of Monmouth's *History*, Arthur's principal knight. He is consistently associated in both traditions with courtesy, but in rather different senses. In the French, he is skilled at what the *Gawain*-poet calls love-talking: this is the reputation that appears to have run ahead of him to Bertilak's castle. In the English, his courtesy shows on a much broader front (such as being particularly kind to novice knights, or, in the *Carl*, covering his host's rain-wet horse with his own cloak), and he combines fearless prowess with the arts of social, rather than sexual, intercourse. The *Gawain*-poet was clearly familiar with both the English and the French traditions, and brings them into dynamic, and slightly comic, opposition in the scenes in the poem in Gawain's bedchamber.

The tone of gentle mockery, even of the mock-heroic, in such scenes has led to the question of whether the romance may not be more of a satire or parody of the genre than a true example. Knights are usually tested in armour on the battlefield rather than naked in bed, as Gawain is, or at least in combat with those dragons and boars that are either dismissed by the poet in half a line or fought by someone other than his hero. Neither the beheading challenge offered at Arthur's court, nor the exchange of winnings proposed by the lord of the castle to which Gawain's quest leads him, ever quite denies its nature as a Christmas game. Gawain, moreover, fails on his quest—or at least, sees

---

[14] The one such episode before Malory occurs in *The Jeaste of Sir Gawain* (?mid-15th cent.; ed. Hahn, pp. 393–418), in which Gawain enjoys a casual affair with the sister of Sir Brandles. There is also a two-line reference to an amatory encounter resulting in the birth of the hero in *Libeaus Desconus*, which may pre-date *Gawain and the Green Knight*, (In the French versions of the stories, the two affairs are the same.)

himself as failing—where it might seem to be a defining charac-
teristic of romance that the knight should succeed.

The same evidence can however be interpreted along lines
almost the opposite of satire. Literary genres are not fixed
taxonomic categories (there is no reliable literary equivalent to
counting a spider's legs to prove that it is not an insect); they are
constructed in terms of conventions, by what is expected or
recognized. If a book begins 'Once upon a time', we expect a
fairy-story and not a scholarly history of the Third Reich; if a
play ends with the death of the major character, we are likely to
take it as a tragedy. In the case of tragedy, exceptionally, we have
a formal definition, from Aristotle's *Poetics*, but there is nothing
comparable for romance. The word 'romance' itself had a wider
range of meanings for much of the Middle Ages than it carries
now, and there was no single term equivalent to the modern
usage. The coherence of the genre, its *recognizability* then and
now, comes from the familiarity of its conventions—from the
settings far away or long ago, in Troy or Camelot; from the
concern with kings, knights, and ladies; from the structure of
aspiration, physically in the form of a quest or ethically in the
form of the pursuit of an ideal; from the almost ubiquitous happy
endings. It was the romance that had set up the secular ideals of
chivalry, and had shown its heroes achieving them—romance is
the genre that insists on the hardest thing of all to make believ-
able, human perfectibility. The *Gawain*-poet, like his great contemporaries Chaucer and Langland, still believes in the ideals;
but, like them, he is unconvinced that human beings can live up
to them. It is commonplace for a knight to commit some kind of
failure early in his quest and then to atone for it and move
beyond it—Chrétien's Perceval himself is the leading example;
but Gawain's discovery of his fault is itself the climactic moment
of his quest, when atonement is not an option within the story.

The familiarity of the building-blocks of romance, in other
words, does not require an author always to build the same
edifice with them. Far more effect can be gained through

surprise or suspense when a writer appears to follow the rules of a genre but in fact breaks them. Shakespeare, in *Hamlet*, takes the standard ingredients of Elizabethan revenge tragedy—a ghost, madness, plenty of corpses along the way and a good heap at the end—but transforms them in a way that ensures that tragedy will never be the same again. The *Gawain*-poet does something similar: he takes the familiar ingredients of an Arthurian setting, a quest, a supernatural antagonist, and a return from apparently unavoidable death, and makes of them something that transforms romance itself.

The poem

The experience of reading *Sir Gawain and the Green Knight* for the first time, when the reader, like Gawain, does not know what is going to happen, is very different from reading it with the hindsight given by knowledge of the plot. Readers who do not know the story are therefore urged to read the poem before continuing with this Introduction.

The contrast between first and second readings follows in part from the poet's pretence of fulfilling romance expectations while in fact doing something rather different, but it is inseparable too from the structure of the poem. Most narratives of chivalric quests, as Gawain's search for the Green Knight is, follow the linear pattern of a journey, from the opening event that inspires the search to its conclusion. Along the way, adventures can be multiplied and digressions followed at the will of the writer. Many of the French Arthurian romances with which the *Gawain*-poet seems to have had some acquaintance complicate the linear structure still further by a process of interlace, where the adventures are followed, not just of a single knight, but of several, in interwoven sequence. In all such romances, there is some kind of conformity of the end to the beginning, as the quest is completed and the knight, or knights, returns to court; but increasingly, from early romance into its Renaissance versions, the digressions can begin to seem more important than the main story, the loops more interesting than the line.

Sir Gawain is radically different. It is set up like many Arthurian romances, with the interruption of a feast by the arrival of a stranger, which will lead to the adventures of the quest itself. Arthur's custom of delaying the start of the meal until some such thing has happened indicates a complicity between character and author in constructing the story: in effect, in such scenes Arthur and his knights act as if they know that they are characters in a romance. In *Sir Gawain*, however, that is the point at which such privileged knowledge stops. The demand for one beheading in return for another may or may not have been familiar to the original audience, but the court itself is utterly unprepared for such a challenge. When the unfathomable, huge, and fashionably dressed Green Knight picks up the head that Gawain has just cut off and demands that he seek him to receive a return blow a year later, the audience or readers may know that he will be safe (not only because of the generic happy ending, but because there are so many other romances that describe his further adventures), but Gawain himself does not. There is, therefore, an important distinction between Gawain's consciousness and the reader's understanding of his situation; yet from the moment that he rides out from Camelot, it is Gawain's point of view that we follow. We may know that he will survive, but we do not know how; and his fears, like the bitter cold of winter he suffers, are described without ironic distance. The central episodes of the romance, when Gawain does no more than lie in bed while his host goes hunting, look like engagingly written but largely unimportant interlace; there are no significant adventures here. Yet when Gawain reaches the place where he is to undergo the return blow—the point of the narrative that should complete his quest—he, and the reader with him, discover that the climax of the story has already passed. The beheading is no longer what matters; it has been overtaken by events that nobody noticed were happening.

The result, in terms of narrative structure, is that the expected linear progression turns out instead to be a mirror symmetry. This is most explicit in the very first and last lines of the poem, with their references to the foundation of Britain after the fall of Troy. Within those references are the scenes at Camelot: Arthur's feast, and Gawain's return. Embedded within the first such scene, and immediately before his return to Camelot at the end, are the specifics of Gawain's kinship: his citation of his uncle Arthur's blood in his body as being the only good thing about him, and the revelation that the old hag is his own aunt, Morgan le Fay. Further inward in the symmetry are Gawain's beheading of the Green Knight, and the Green Knight's reciprocal near-beheading of Gawain. The initial scene of arming, culminating in the shield with its badge of the pentangle, and followed by Gawain's first, unguided, journey, is matched by the second arming, when the final item that he dons is the green girdle, and his riding out with the guide to find the Green Chapel. At the centre of the whole structure are the three bedroom scenes and the hunts: scenes that represent, not rest and recuperation on Gawain's part and an addiction to the aristocratic pastime of hunting on the lord's, but the pursuit of a single quarry—Gawain himself—with potentially deadly consequences.

Each episode in the second half of the poem comments on its counterpart in the first half. Gawain steps forward to claim the adventure from among a young and untested court, with a speech of meticulous courtesy and elaborate humility; he returns sadder, wiser and deeply humiliated. His kinship with Arthur had seemed a guarantee of excellence, of everything that separates the civilization of the court from the huge and alien green figure who disrupts the feast; his equal kinship with Morgan insists that, whatever it is that the Green Knight represents, it is as deeply in his blood as Arthur's courtliness and nobility. On the first journey, his worst problems are not the dragons and wild beasts customary in romances, which are dealt with in little more than a parenthesis, but the physical trials of the winter weather; on the second journey, to the Green Chapel itself, he is suddenly given the chance to escape, a test of ethical integrity rather than physical endurance all the sharper for being unexpected. He insists on going on to receive the return blow, expecting it to be a test of physical courage and the issue solely one of survival, as it had appeared at Arthur's court; he discovers that the stakes have been changed completely in the scenes in the bedroom that seemed to have nothing to do with it, that his fate has been decided while he was not looking. Despite his unawareness, he already carries on him the sign of his failure—the lady's girdle, which he has put on over his coat-armour of the pentangle: a lace that can be knotted and untied to replace the 'endless knot' of the pentangle itself.

Just what it is that Gawain does wrong has none the less been a matter of some controversy. It has been suggested that his acceptance of a magic talisman contravenes his initial consent to the return blow; certainly such supernatural assistance was forbidden in judicial combats, but the argument is hard to sustain when the Green Knight himself can survive beheading —the girdle might seem to make the odds between them more even, less unfair. More explicit as potential areas of failure are the virtues symbolized by the pentangle Gawain carries on his shield, and which he proclaims to the world as his chivalric code: the virtues of generosity, good fellowship, purity, courtesy, and *pité*, piety or compassion.[15] When the wife of his host sets about trying to seduce him, he is anxious that he will not be able to maintain his sexual integrity (his purity) or his duties to his host (good fellowship) unless he breaches his courtesy to the lady; but he does in fact manage to preserve all three virtues. After the Green Knight has revealed his identity, Gawain accuses himself

---

[15] For further discussion of the pentangle and its virtues, see the Explanatory Note to p. 24, and also N. M. Davis, 'Gawain's Rationalist Pentangle', *Arthurian Literature*, 12 (1993), 37–62. For an argument that it represents righteousness, see Gerald Morgan, *Sir Gawain and the Green Knight and the Idea of Righteousness* (Blackrock, 1991).

of a string of vices including covetousness (the sin opposed to generosity) and cowardice; but they are not charges that Bertilak appears to agree with.

One alternative to seeking out Gawain's transgressions of his code lies in emphasizing instead the religious significance given to the pentangle, and to the image of the Virgin painted on the inside of the shield. By this argument, Gawain shows a failure of faith, since at the moment of crisis he puts his trust in a talisman, the lady's green girdle, not in Christ or in Mary. The Green Knight by this reading becomes in some sense a figure for God, or at least someone who pronounces a quasi-divine judgement on Gawain. The cycle of the year contained in the poem runs (more or less) from Advent, the first coming of the Lord that prefigures his Second Coming at the Last Judgement, through to a second Advent when a kind of judgement is indeed about to happen. New Year's Day is also the Feast of Circumcision, one of the many occasions in the liturgical year associated with penitence; and it has been argued that the wound in Gawain's neck is intended to evoke the associations of circumcision.[16] It has to be said, however, that medieval poets who write religious allegory generally make it very clear that they are doing so, and that if such a reading were correct, the poet here is going out of his way to conceal it. New Year's Day is the only date in the poem that is defined in terms of the secular rather than the liturgical calendar; and neither Gawain nor the Green Knight ever mentions the possibility that Gawain's failure might be a religious one in so sharply defined a sense. The wound on his neck is more obviously taken as a variation on the *colée*, the blow on the neck (not, as now, on the shoulder) that constituted the defining moment in the ceremony of creating a knight: it symbolizes penance for a chivalric failure, not for a failure of piety. If the castle, the scene of Gawain's temptation, does indeed appear in

---

[16] R. A. Shoaf, *The Poem as Green Girdle: Commercium in Sir Gawain and the Green Knight* (Gainesville, Fl., 1984).

answer to his prayer for somewhere to hear Mass at Christmas, then the Virgin has a very mordant sense of humour in answering prayers. It is true that she was held to be the primary intercessor on behalf of one's soul; but Gawain, for better or worse, is most intent on saving his life. That does not indicate a saintly set of priorities—covetousness, of which he accuses himself, could in medieval theological definitions include too great an attachment to life, though the standard lay penitential handbooks define the sin in rather more wordly terms—but neither Gawain nor the poet ever suggests that his desire for self-preservation is wrong, and the Green Knight actively denies it.

Alternative interpretations of the Green Knight suggested within the poem itself might seem to exonerate Gawain from any blame, though there is a slipperiness to those interpretations that suggests that Bertilak is as adept a shape-shifter in meaning as in outward form. (He is indeed unique in English romance in that his primary shape is never finally determined: just as it seems clear that he is really Sir Bertilak, he rides off, not back to his castle in his human shape, but 'wherever he would', and still green.) Gawain suspects him of being the devil; but that is demonstrably wrong, since in his other form, as lord of the castle, he attends Mass assiduously, as no one with diabolic connections could do. Nor is the temptation he imposes on Gawain a religious one: it is a test of Christian knightly virtues, but not directly of piety or faith such as would happen in a saint's life. When Perceval, in the Vulgate version of the Grail, is approached by a beautiful woman who tells him how much she desires him, she turns out to be the devil in disguise; and the Grail quest, moreover, is one for which virginity, on the model of the saint, is the primary qualification. Female saints were often the object of sexual approaches, but normally with a concomitant demand to abandon their faith. The poet describes the Virgin as taking an active interest in protecting Gawain's sexual purity, but there is no suggestion that the requirements of celibate sanctity operate in the poem; and Mary does not get any mention in the final confrontation of Gawain and the Green Knight, nor on his return to court.

An alternative suggestion made within the poem is that the Green Knight is a personification of death. Death is the one encounter common to everyone; he himself notes that Gawain cannot fail to find him, and the guide insists that no one from any division of society can escape alive from a meeting with him. The very fact that Gawain survives his encounter, however, as well as the Green Knight's delight in his survival and his huge zest for life, make it clear that these apparent clues are designed more to scare Gawain than to inform the reader. The opposite interpretation was strenuously argued a few decades ago, that not only was the Green Knight a symbol of life, but the whole poem was a latter-day vegetation myth with its sources and origins in continuing pagan practices. The setting of the poem at the cusp of the Old and New Year, the Green Knight's greenness, the evergreen holly that he carries, and his survival of decapitation were all called on as proof. Attractive as the idea may be, it owes far more to twentieth-century desires for mythic origins than to any plausible medieval context.[17] The 'green man' sometimes cited as a close relation of the Green Knight has almost nothing in common with the figure in the poem: frequently appearing in church carvings in the fourteenth and fifteenth centuries, it takes the form of a face emerging from, or merging into, surrounding foliage, with tendrils growing out of its mouth. It has no body, no fine clothes, no greenness except what the onlooker projects onto it, no habitation, and no known myth or legend attaching to it.[18] This need not mean, however, that modern tendencies to perceive mythic significances in the

---

[17] The idea was forcefully argued by John Speirs, in a 1949 essay incorporated into his *Medieval English Poetry: The Non-Chaucerian Tradition* (London, 1957), 215–51; he cited the mummers' plays of decapitation and the figure of the Jack-in-the-green as supporting evidence. Far from being ancient traditions, however, these originated centuries after the poem: see Ronald Hutton, *The Stations of the Sun: A History of the Ritual Year in Britain* (Oxford, 1996), esp. 70–80, 241–2.

[18] See Kathleen Basford, *The Green Man* (Ipswich, 1978).

text are as misguided as the medieval custom of reading Ovid's *Metamorphoses* for its allegories of Christian doctrine. An alertness to the possibilities of linking the New Year with death and the renewal of life is explicit in the narrative, and there is no need to deny so highly intelligent a poet an awareness of the potential of his own story. It is by no means uncommon for the hero or heroine of a romance to undergo some kind of symbolic resurrection, to return from apparent death—Shakespeare's romances are full of such things; but the *Gawain*-poet makes the motif part of a nexus with the cycle of the year, with sex (in the bedroom scenes) and death (in the hunts as well as the challenge), and with the unexplained greenness and vigour of the man who can walk off with his head in his hand on New Year's Day. The Green Knight may not be a verbal equivalent of the stone green men, but some kind of punning relationship between them in the poet's imagination remains entirely possible. The colour green in the Middle Ages has almost too many associations—with death and the devil, and also with fairies, jealousy, inconstancy, and faithfulness, among many other things.[19] Its most obvious association, however, is with life; and life in turn carries with it the implication of mortality.

Whatever the Green Knight represents, at the end of the poem he pronounces a judgement inseparable from the ethics of Christian knighthood, and Gawain's fault is a breach of those principles. Bertilak himself indicates where Gawain's catastrophic failure occurs, though the moment at which he transgressed is so silent that on first reading it is easy to overlook. The identity he proclaims to the world through the sum total of the virtues of the pentangle is one of *trawthe*, truth—a word that combines the ideas of truth (what is true, fixed and stable), troth (faith to one's plighted word), and integrity (truth to one's self). In the other poems of the Cotton manuscript, the word is often used for those qualities such as righteousness and truth-telling

[19] See Derek Brewer, 'The Colour Green', Brewer and Gibson, 181–90.

that humankind can share with God; the *Gawain*-poet's two great contemporaries, Chaucer and Langland, go so far as to use the word as a periphrasis for God Himself. The pentangle, symbol of the virtues, the perfection of the senses, and the five wounds of Christ, is a 'token of truth' that epitomizes all these meanings. Once he has ridden out from Camelot, however, Gawain is so intent on fulfilling his promise to the Green Knight, keeping *trawthe* with him, that he apparently does not notice that he has given his word again in the game Bertilak sets up with him the following Christmas, to exchange whatever each wins on three successive days. His failure to keep his word, to hand over the girdle given him by the lady, results in his injury when it is his turn to receive the blow from the axe; and he accordingly describes the girdle as the 'token of untruth' that demonstrates his guilt. The sin in itself may be venial, as the Green Knight suggests when he congratulates Gawain on his closeness to perfection when compared to other knights; but to Gawain, any fall from the perfection of truth is absolute.

Gawain's keeping of the girdle is structurally as well as ethically problematic. It is extremely difficult to make a hero who carries a magic talisman appear heroic: there would be nothing striking left about Gawain's bravery if he knew he had nothing to fear. The poet treads the line brilliantly between seeming to provide a means by which the romance might yet end happily, and not allowing the girdle to solve all the problems. Gawain takes the girdle in the hope rather than the belief that it may save him, as the subjunctives in his reaction to being offered it indicate—that it *might be* a talisman to preserve his life, *maybe* death *could* be foiled. His lack of faith in it is indicated by the appalling night he spends before he rides out to the Green Chapel, counting the hours and unable to sleep, despite his care to tie it round himself in the morning. It would not seem to have any possible role when he is standing before the man with the huge axe, and it never enters his thoughts until the Green Knight calls attention to it. The lady had promised that he would not be killed while he is wearing it, and he is not killed; yet there must be very few readers who would believe the lady's word rather than her husband's statement that if he had not taken it he would not even have been hurt—that it is the cause of his injury, not of his survival. In other romances, the wonder aroused by magic or the supernatural can be transferred to the hero when his own love or bravery turns out to surpass whatever the supposed magic can offer. In the romance of *Floris and Blaunche-flour*, for instance, a ring that promises survival saves both protagonists when, condemned to death by a pagan emir who loves Blauncheflour and has found the lovers in bed together, they each try to give it to the other, drop it, and so reveal the full strength of their love—whereupon the emir is so moved that he spares them. The ring does not act in magical fashion, but its possession of such powers is never questioned. The lady's girdle, by contrast, turns out, so far as we know, to be an entirely ordinary one; and its existence measures not the hero's excep-tional qualities, as Floris's ring shows his love to be stronger than his fear of death, but Gawain's common humanity, his falli-bility.[20]

The Green Knight's explanation of the girdle and its role pulls the whole romance into shape. It brings the quest into significant relationship with those lingered-on central scenes in the bedroom; it is the defining moment for showing that the mirror symmetry is not just one of event but of moral import too. Yet Bertilak adds in a further item of explanation that is in-creasingly baffling the more one thinks about it: Morgan le Fay. It is she, he claims, who turned him green, and who sent him to test Arthur's court and to scare Guinevere to death. Such powers, and such motives, would be in keeping with the pre-sentation of Morgan in other Arthurian romances, and in that sense they do indeed seem to provide a rationale for everything that has happened. But as an attempt to murder Guinevere, the

[20] See Helen Cooper, 'The Supernatural', Brewer and Gibson, 285–91.

events at court were singularly inept and unsuccessful; and the
Green Knight never claims that Morgan had anything to do with
the testing of Gawain—it is he himself who set his wife to woo
him. Nor does he claim Morgan's assistance in turning green
again at the end, and it is indeed difficult to imagine him as
under her thumb. John Speirs famously suggested that Morgan
is in the poem simply as 'a bone for the rationalizing mind to
play with, and to be kept quiet with';[21] but the shadowy, unexplained, and insidious presence of the hideous old woman implies something more than that. One way to define her function
in the poem must be in terms of the poem's symmetries, with
their insistence that her blood-relationship to Gawain is as close
as his much-vaunted relationship to Arthur. It may even have
been that duality in Gawain, the most perfect of Arthur's knights
in the English tradition, the model of courtesy but with an equal
share in his blood of the darkness represented by Morgan, that
suggested the story in the first place. Gawain is not evil
—Bertilak serves as a buffer between the knight and his aunt,
and makes the testing of Gawain's virtue finally more sympa-
thetic than hostile—but even for this most famous of knights,
perfection is not an option.

To think of the poem in terms of exemplary perfection and its
failure is to emphasize its ethical concerns. It was axiomatic in
the Middle Ages, and for long afterwards, that fiction with any
pretension to value must instruct as well as entertain: poetry was
often classified as a subsection of ethics. Fallibility is an inevit-
able human attribute; despite Gawain's mention of Adam, the
poet does not explicitly define it in theological terms, as original
sin, but Gawain is unmistakably a character from a fallen world.
That does not mean, however, that ideals are delusory. Without
the pentangle to set his standards by, Gawain would presumably
have failed much more drastically; and failure itself is better than
not trying at all. Writing most of three centuries later, but

---

[21] Speirs, *Medieval English Poetry*, 218.

commenting on what one could learn from the reading of romance quests, John Milton insisted that the grime picked up in the course of experience was better than the purity of never having been exposed:

I cannot praise a fugitive and cloistered virtue, unexercized and unbreathed, that never sallies out and sees her adversary, but slinks out of the race, where that immortal garland is to be run for, not without dust and heat. Assuredly we bring not innocence into the world, we bring impurity much rather: that which purifies us is trial, and trial is by what is contrary.[22]

That is why Gawain's humiliation on his return to court seems so much more ethically satisfying than his earlier declaration of worthlessness, and why the other members of the court, who have kept themselves safely out of temptation's way, seem so superficial at the end, despite their acknowledgement, closely parallel to Sir Bertilak's, of the nobility of Gawain's achievement.

The poetics of Sir Gawain and the Green Knight

Sir Gawain and the Green Knight works by different poetic principles from any recent poetry. As an amplification of Keith Harrison's account of his solutions to the problems posed by a modern verse translation of such a work, a description of the poetics of the original text may be useful.[23]

The work belongs to the fourteenth-century poetic movement known as the 'Alliterative Revival'—'alliterative', because the defining feature of the poems of the movement is the repetition of key sounds within each line, rather than rhyme or a strictly

---

[22] *Areopagitica* (1644) (numerous editions; p. 213 in the Penguin *John Milton: Selected Prose* ed. C. A. Patrides (Harmondsworth, 1974)). The romance Milton cites as demonstrating the process is Book II of Spenser's *Faerie Queene*.

[23] The classic study is by Marie Borroff, *Sir Gawain and the Green Knight: A Stylistic and Metrical Study* (New Haven, 1962).

regular metrical pattern; 'revival', because Old English poetry had employed a closely similar verse form, but it had disappeared, at least from the written record, over the centuries since the Norman Conquest. The poems of the Alliterative Revival share with each other a similar line structure, and often also similar vocabulary and phrasing. They were all written in the north or west of England or in southern Scotland, and a number beside the *Gawain*-poet's own works belong to the Staffordshire–Cheshire area; but their writers did not constitute a 'school' in the sense of knowing each other and encouraging each other's work. The earliest texts of the Revival date probably from the mid-fourteenth century, the latest from the early sixteenth.

Old English verse had generally employed a strict alliterative scheme, in which each line had four stressed syllables, two in each half-line with a caesura in the middle. The two stresses of the first half-line, and the first stress of the second half, all began with the same sound: a form that can be represented schematically as AA / A*(x)*, A representing the alliterating sounds and *(x)* the 'wild' sound, as Keith Harrison calls it. The unstressed syllables of the line fell around these in a narrow range of permitted metrical patterns. The poetry of the Alliterative Revival uses a longer line, again with a caesura in the middle, but with more permissive patterns of both alliteration and rhythm. The opening lines of *Sir Gawain and the Green Knight* illustrate many of the kinds of variations that the *Gawain*-poet uses. (A slash marks the mid-line breaks; some manuscripts of alliterative poems mark these by the use of a point, but the *Gawain* scribe does not.)

Sithen the sege and the assaut / watz sesed at Troye,
The borgh brittened and brent / to brondez and askez,
The tulk that the trammes / of tresoun ther wroght
Watz tried for his tricherie, / the trewest on erthe,
Hit watz Ennias the athel, / and his highe kynde,
That sithen depreced provinces, / and patrounes bicome
Welneghe of al the wele / in the west iles.

The passage introduces the virtuoso skill that characterizes the entire poem. The first two lines offer not two but three alliterating syllables in the first half-line: sithen—sege—assaut ('assault', stressed on the second syllable) / sesed, with the last stressed syllable, 'Troye', as its 'wild' sound; borgh—brittened —brent / brondez, with 'askez' as its 'wild' sound. The third and fourth lines represent the classic AA / A*(x)* form of the alliterative line, but here enriched by running the same sound, t- or tr-, across both lines: tulk—trammes / tresoun; tried—tricherie / trewest. The fifth line shows another standard variation permitted in alliterative poetry, that all vowels and initial h- alliterate together. The alliterating words are therefore hit (lightly stressed, like 'sithen' in the first line)—Ennais —athel / highe (the three chief stresses). In the next line, 'sithen' again carries a light stress, but this time it is 'wild' (the chief alliterating stresses are depreced—provinces / patrounes). In the last line, unusually, the alliterating letter opens the line, welnigh—wele / west; but the second stressed sound, the vowel of 'al', offers a secondary alliteration with the final 'iles'. Even this range of examples is far from exhausting the poet's variants, however. He will sometimes alliterate on all four stresses in a line:

> They boghen bi bonkkez / ther boghes ar bare,
> Thay clomben bi clyffes / ther clengez the colde. (2077–8)

And there are numerous other variations too, which are a matter not just of technical differences but of rhetorical effect, to emphasize some words or phrases, and, always, to keep the shape and sound of the line perpetually surprising, always offering something new.

It is a pattern which is much easier to hear than to describe; reading aloud is strongly recommended—and indeed, like all medieval vernacular literature, the poem was written to be heard rather than just to be read on the page. (An instant, improperly simplified, guide to reading the original aloud is to adopt a

Yorkshire accent to broaden the vowels, and to pronounce all the letters: 'knyght' sounds both the initial k, and the -gh- (like the -ch in Scottish 'loch'); its plural, 'knyghtes', has two syllables). The proportion of the fourteenth-century population who could read was still comparatively small, but it required only one literate person in a group to be able to read aloud to the others; silent reading did not become the norm until very much later. The fact that in long winter evenings there might be only one adequate source of light in a room to read by, as well as the lack of any mass production of manuscripts, ensured that reading aloud was a common form of entertainment. The rhythms of *Sir Gawain and the Green Knight* are brilliantly effective for conveying the maximum excitement within the discipline of the spoken line.

There is one feature of the poem which is distinctly unusual, and that is the rhyming 'bob and wheel' (the phrase was devised by nineteenth-century editors) that close each verse—the short, usually two-syllable line with a single stress, and the four three-stress lines that follow. The three-stress lines usually also contain alliteration, sometimes on all the stressed syllables, though it is less of a requirement than in the long verse lines. The bob and wheel has the functions of providing further rhythmical variation, and of dividing the narrative up: the poet will often use the wheel to provide some kind of summary, of the action past or in hand or occasionally to come—

> Now thenk well, Sir Gawan,
> For wothe that thou ne wonde
> This aventure for to frayn
> That thou hatz tan on honde.   (487–90)

The combination of conciseness and rhyme sets a translator the hardest challenge.

The verse form of the poem can be represented in a translation, even if the task is not easy. The poet's word choice, by contrast, and the range of his vocabulary, are impossible to reproduce in modern English without sounding intolerably precious or archaic. He had at his disposal the Old English-derived words that form the common stock of the language; a handful of words adopted from Norse, the language of the Viking invaders; a wide vocabulary of French-derived words that were pouring through from Anglo-Norman into English in the late fourteenth century, and which carried with them a strong aristocratic or courtly charge; and a range of words that are rarely found outside alliterative poetry, and for which he often provides the last or near-to-last recorded usage in English. Words of this last group frequently figure as synonyms for terms for which there is a constant need, such as 'man' or 'knight'. For these, it is immensely useful to have a range of words to hand that start with whatever letter a line may require; and so, while the commonplace 'man' frequently appears at the end of a line where alliteration is not required, half an alphabet of less usual words can be called on to fit the demands of the alliteration—burne, freke, gome, hathel, leude, schalk, segge, tulk, and wyghe, besides 'man' and 'knight' themselves. These uncommon words were presumably poetically marked—that is, they were immediately recognizable as belonging to a higher register than ordinary prose writing or speech. (By contrast, the synonyms for 'man' in modern English are almost all of a lower, more colloquial register—bloke, chap, fellow, guy.) The language of the poem therefore has a richness of resonance that cannot be reproduced in modern English, because its unusual words have now been either lost altogether or so assimilated into the language as to cease to surprise, and because those different layers of vocabulary—the tough monosyllabic Old English, the more elaborate courtly French—have become so mixed as largely to have lost their different textures and associations.

One feature of the layout of the text should also be mentioned, and that is its division into four parts. Despite the pseudo-medieval appearance conferred on this scheme by calling the four sections 'fitts', as many modern editions do, it in fact originates with the first printed edition of the text, in the mid-nineteenth century. The manuscript does indicate structural divisions at these points, but by the use of large decorated initial letters rather than by numbers or subheadings. Moreover, similar but slightly smaller initials also occur at the start of the description of the pentangle, the discovery of the castle, the boar-hunt, the killing of the fox, and the return blow. In this edition, the customary editorial section numbers are retained, though without the headings, and the decorated initials are indicated typographically.

TRANSLATOR'S NOTE

The first and last thing that a translator has to keep in mind when working on *Sir Gawain and the Green Knight* is that it is a rattling good story. Tempo, tone, diction, and the sound of characters actually speaking are therefore of signal importance. The second, and no less important thing is that it is in verse. Not metre, to be sure, but the kind of verse that was put to sleep, almost permanently, by the genius of Chaucer who, by borrowing his models from Italian and French verse, turned English poetry into something European as well as English. This poem, though it does have a strong French element, is part of a revival of a much older English tradition of 'telling' which has very little to do with the music of metrical verse. The structure of this poem—with its repeated pattern of 'stock', 'bob' and 'wheel', as well as its very heavily accented alliterations along the verse-line—requires a different kind of ear from the one we bring to Chaucer or to the blank verse of Shakespeare, whose especial and utterly different virtues hardly need defending.

In trying to win over this remarkable poem into modern English I was therefore determined to put it into modern narrative verse. But what kind of verse? After experimenting for some time, I remembered certain passages in *Four Quartets* where T. S. Eliot, the quintessential modernist, goes back to the old native tradition and composes his lines—as Dame Helen Gardner has shown in her brilliant essay on Eliot's verse —around 'blows' or stresses, not metrical feet. This seemed a good place to begin. Yet I also wanted to preserve a strong ghost of the alliterative texture of Middle English verse, a subliminal sound-pattern, as it were, and to do that without foregrounding the music of the poem at the expense of its meaning. To mimic the heavy stresses of the original in any literal way meant taking the risk, in a modern version, of sounding archaic or, at least, very odd. Pound might have got away with that kind of experiment in his version of *The Seafarer*, but by the time he came to write *The Cantos* the music of his verse had changed considerably: he had transmuted our traditional ideas of alliteration and assonance into a very flexible, yet very modern, instrument of poetic expressiveness.

The solution arrived at in my own case was to modify the original sound-structure by using not one single repeated sound in each line but *two* pairs of like sounds, with the aim of producing in the ear a kind of dynamic shuttling. In the original there are, though not with absolute regularity, five 'blows' to the line. Three, or more often four, of those blows occur on the same sound. Here are two typical lines:

```
(x)       /           /         /          (x)
```
Fyrst he clad him in his clothes, the colde for to were   (2015)

```
/         /          /         /       (x)
```
Bothe wyth bulles and beres and bores otherquyle   (722)

In the first, there are two 'wild' sounds *(x)* that do not belong to the alliterative pattern, but are still stressed by the speaking voice. The other three stresses in that line all occur on the same consonant. In the second example, four of the stressed sounds occur on the same consonant and only one stressed sound is 'wild'.

My point of departure was this second kind of line. Obviously, two pairs can be arranged in any of three ways.

1. A A B B
2. A B B A
3. A B A B

There remains the 'wild' sound *(x)*. In the original, it normally occurs on the last stressed sound of the line, as in the first example above. For the sake of variation, I decided to let it occur anywhere in the line. Here, then, is an example of each of the three new patterns, taken in the above order:

    A   (x)   A   B   B
 1. *It's clear there's no one here but beardless boys.*   (280)

    A B   (x)   B   A
 2. *His wide beard glistened like a beaver's hide.*   (845)

    A   B   A   (x) B
 3. *Where plummeting cascades from the summits ran cold . . .*
(731)

There are some minor variants. Sometimes one has the luck to find a word that comprehends the two sounds one is looking for. For instance, the word '*beardless*' in the first example echoes both the '*b*' of its companion '*boys*', as well as the assonance of '*clear*' and '*here*'. One accepts such gifts gladly, especially when a whole line sounds like something that could occur quite naturally in modern speech. In a handful of cases the demands of the text generated such difficulties that I had, very reluctantly, to accept a compromise. In the main, though, I have tried to stick to the three patterns shown above.

It hardly needs to be added that I hope a reader will not be conscious of these technicalities while reading the poem. I wanted most of all, in spite of them, and because of them, to make a version that could be read to a modern audience—over the radio, in a theatre, to a group of children—and sound as natural as possible. *Sir Gawain* is predominantly an oral poem; it must be spoken, or intoned. It is not a poem for the eye. And, just as the tone of the poem is varied, so is the language. Francis Berry, among others, has emphasized the jagged and sinewy quality of the original.[1] I think it is important to add that it also

---

1 *The Age of Chaucer* (Baltimore, 1954), 148–58.

has moments of great lyrical beauty, and flashes of irony and sly humour, and these modulations, which can only be fully captured by the speaking voice, provide a fascinating challenge for the translator.

For many of us *Sir Gawain* is as alive today as it was six hundred years ago. Good stories do not age and, like most translators, I wanted to celebrate the essential and enduring life of my text. But I also wanted to produce an accurate version. If I have succeeded in any measure in this double aim and, in so doing, turned my readers to a study of the original, I shall consider all the labour worthwhile. My overall debt to Ezra Pound in this work will, I think, be quite apparent. If not, I acknowledge it now. About translation, about the art of verse in all its aspects, he has taught many of us most of what we know.

SELECT BIBLIOGRAPHY

I. *Editions*

Anderson, J. J., ed., *Sir Gawain and the Green Knight, Pearl, Cleanness and Patience* (London, 1996).

Andrew, Malcolm, and Waldron, Ronald, eds., *The Poems of the Pearl Manuscript* (2nd rev. edn., Exeter, 1996).

Tolkien, J. R. R., and Gordon, E. V., eds., *Sir Gawain and the Green Knight*, 2nd edn. rev. Norman Davis (Oxford, 1967).

II. *Criticism*

Benson, Larry D., *Art and Tradition in Sir Gawain and the Green Knight* (New Brunswick, NJ, 1965).

Borroff, Marie, *Sir Gawain and the Green Knight: A Stylistic and Metrical Study* (New Haven, 1962).

Brewer, Derek, and Gibson, Jonathan, eds., *A Companion to the Gawain-Poet* (Cambridge, 1997).

Brewer, Elisabeth, *Sir Gawain and the Green Knight: Sources and Analogues* (2nd edn., Cambridge, 1992).

Burrow, J. A., *A Reading of Sir Gawain and the Green Knight* (London, 1965).

—— *Ricardian Poetry: Chaucer, Gower, Langland and the 'Gawain' Poet* (London, 1971).

Davis, N. M., 'Gawain's Rationalist Pentangle', *Arthurian Literature*, 12 (1993), 37–62.

Howard, D. R., and Zacher, C., eds., *Critical Studies of Sir Gawain and the Green Knight* (London, 1968).

Mann, Jill, 'Price and Value in *Sir Gawain and the Green Knight*', *Essays in Criticism*, 36 (1986), 294–328.

Morgan, Gerald, *Sir Gawain and the Green Knight and the Idea of Righteousness* (Blackrock, 1991).

Putter, Ad, *An Introduction to the Gawain-Poet* (London and New York, 1996).

—— *Sir Gawain and the Green Knight and French Arthurian Romance* (Oxford, 1995).

Spearing, A. C., *The Gawain-Poet: A Critical Study* (Cambridge, 1970).

III. *Cultural and Social Background*

Barber, Richard, *The Knight and Chivalry* (rev. edn., Woodbridge, 1995).

Bennett, Michael J., *Community, Class and Careerism: Cheshire and Lancashire Society in the Age of Sir Gawain and the Green Knight* (Cambridge, 1983).

—— 'Courtly Literature and Northwest England in the Later Middle Ages', in *Court and Poet*, ed. Glyn S. Burgess and others (Liverpool, 1981), 69–78.

Caxton, William, trans., *The Book of the Ordre of Chivalry*, ed. A. T. P. Byles, Early English Text Society OS 168 (1926).

Chaucer, Geoffrey, *The Riverside Chaucer*, ed. Larry D. Benson (Oxford, 1988).

Chrétien de Troyes, *Arthurian Romances*, trans. W. W. Kibler (Harmondsworth, 1991).

Hahn, Thomas, ed., *Sir Gawain: Eleven Romances and Tales* (Kalamazoo, Mich., 1995).

Keen, Maurice, *Chivalry* (New Haven, 1984).

Rooney, Anne, *Hunting in Middle English Literature* (Cambridge, 1993).

Turville-Petre, T., *The Alliterative Revival* (Cambridge and Totowa, NJ, 1977).

CHRONOLOGY

The *Gawain*-poet was writing some time before 1400, the latest date for the copying of his works into the one surviving manuscript, and probably after 1370. The chronology below outlines some of the political, literary, and social events of his hypothetical lifetime.

1337	Start of the Hundred Years War with France
?1340	Birth of Geoffrey Chaucer
1342	Birth of Julian of Norwich
1348	Order of the Garter founded
1348–9	Black Death
?1350s	Early works of the Alliterative Revival
1356	Battle of Poitiers
1361	Jean Froissart begins work on his *Chroniques*
1362	John of Gaunt becomes Duke of Lancaster
?1368	Chaucer's *Book of the Duchess*
	A-text of William Langland's *Piers Plowman*
1369	Resumption of war with France
1372–3	Chaucer's first visit to Italy
1374	Death of Petrarch
1376	Death of the Black Prince
1377	Death of Edward III; accession of Richard II
	Death of Guillaume de Machaut
?1380	B-text of Langland's *Piers Plowman*
1381	Peasants' Revolt
1384	Death of John Wyclif
?1386	Chaucer's *Troilus and Criseyde*
	Death of Langland
1386–1400	Chaucer's *Canterbury Tales*
1387	Richard II visits Cheshire
1388	Merciless Parliament
c. 1389	Gaston Phébus' *Livre de Chasse*
1390	Richard II first uses the badge of the White Hart
	John Gower's *Confession amantis*
c. 1390	Wycliffite translation of the Bible

[xlv]

SIR GAWAIN AND THE
GREEN KNIGHT

I

AFTER the battle and the attack were over at Troy,
  The town beaten down to smoking brands and ashes,
  That man enmeshed in the nets of treachery—the truest
Of men—was tried for treason; I mean
Aeneas, the high-born,* who, with his noble kinsmen,
Conquered many countries and made themselves masters
Of almost all the wealth of the Western Isles.*
Romulus goes off in haste towards Rome, raises
At first that fine city with pride, bestowing
On her his famous name, which she still has now.   10
Ticius builds new towns in Tuscany
And Langeberde lays out homes in Lombardy
And, joyfully, far over the French sea,
Felix Brutus founds Britain* by ample down
          and bay;
      Where war, and joy, and terror
      Have all at times held sway;
      Where both delight and horror
      Have had their fitful day.

And after Britain was founded by this brave fighter   20
Rough fellows were fathered here who relished a fray
And made much mischief in troubled times.
More marvels have occurred in this country*
Than any other since then, so far as I know.
But of all the kings who've commanded this land
Men say King Arthur was the greatest in courtesy.

[3]

Let me tell you, then, a tale of adventure,
A most striking one among the marvels of Arthur
Which some will consider a wonder to hear.
If you listen closely to my words a little while   30
I'll tell it to you now as I heard it told
        in town:
    A bold story, well proven,
    And everywhere well known,
    The letters all interwoven
    As custom sets it down.*

Christmas time. The king is home at Camelot
Among his many lords, all splendid men—
All the trusted brothers of the Round Table
Ready for court revels and carefree pleasures.   40
Knights in great numbers at the tournament sports
Jousted with much joy, as gentle knights
Will do, then rode to the court for the carol-dances.*
The festival lasted fifteen long days*
Of great mirth with all the meat that they could manage.
Such clamour and merriment were amazing to hear:
By day a joyful noise, dancing at night—
A happiness that rang through rooms and halls
With lords and ladies pleasing themselves as they pleased.
So in delight they lived and danced there together: 50
The knights of highest renown under Christ Himself,
The loveliest ladies that ever on earth drew breath,
The handsomest king that ever kept court,
All in that hall were beautiful, young and, of
        their kind,
    The happiest under heaven,

A king of powerful mind;
A company so proven
Would now be hard to find.

With the New Year so young it had hardly begun,   60
Those seated at the dais* were given double servings.
Then, when the sound of the chanting in the chapel subsided,
The king came with all his knights to the hall
And loud cries leapt out from clerics and laymen:
'Noel!' they shouted, again and again 'Noel!'*
Then noble knights ran forward with New Year gifts,*
Handed out what they had, shouting, with loud
Guessing-games about each other's gifts.
Even when they guessed wrong the ladies laughed—
And, believe me, those who won weren't angry at all.   70
This merrymaking took place before the meal.
When they had washed* they took their tables
In their right ranks, highest first, as was fitting.
Queen Guinevere, the gayest of all the gathering,
Sat at the high dais which was hung with adornments,
A canopy over her, silken curtains all round:
Damasks of Toulouse and rich drapes from Turkestan*
Sewn and set off by the most detailed designs
In rich metals and jewels, beautifully beaten
                    and wrought—   80
     No woman lovelier,
     Her grey eyes* glancing about;
     In beauty she had no peer,
     Of that there was no doubt.

But Arthur refused to eat till the rest were served.

He was in merry mood, like a mischievous boy.
He liked a life of action and couldn't abide
Long stretches of lying about or sitting idle;
His blood burned, his restless mind roused him.
But that day he was driven by a different resolve;   90
He had nobly decided never to eat at feasts
Such as these, until someone had told him
A strange story or a splendid adventure*—
Something marvellous and beautiful that he might believe,
With the clamour of battle, attacks, the clash of arms—
Or till someone entreated him to spare a knight
To join with in jousting, jeopardizing their limbs
And even their lives on the field, yielding advantage
As the favours of fortune touched the luckier one.
Such was Arthur's new custom with his court,   100
At feasts and festivals, with the fine company
              in his hall.
        So now, in his kingly way,
        He stands fearless and tall,
        Alert on that New Year's Day,
        And jests among them all.

In this regal manner he remains for quite a while
Talking of courtly trifles before the High Table
Where the knight, Gawain, is next to Guinevere,
With Agravain a la Dure Main at the other side—   110
Both sons of the king's sister, trusted brother knights.
Bishop Baldwin is head of the High Table
With Iwain, Urien's son,* to keep him company.
All these are seated and served with honour
And likewise those on the long side-tables.

The first course comes with a burst of trumpets
Whose banners hung from them in brilliant colours.
And now a clatter of kettledrums, a chiffing of fifes:
Wild music that ricochets off walls and rafters;
And the listeners' hearts leap with the lively notes.   120
Costly and most delicious foods are carried in:
Great mounds of steaming meat—so many dishes
There's little space in front of the lords and ladies
To set all the heaped silver platters that rapidly
       appear.
    Each man eats as he wishes,
    Lustily takes his share;
    Each pair has twelve full dishes,*
    Bright wine, and foaming beer.

Well, I won't tell you more about the meal;   130
You can be sure, of course, there was little lacking.
But now another sound was stirring—one
Which would allow the king to come and dine.
The first course had barely been served
To all the court, the music hardly hushed,
When there hove into the hall a hideous figure,
Square-built and bulky, full-fleshed from neck to thigh:
The heaviest horseman in the world, the tallest as well,
His loins and limbs so large and so long
I think he may have been half-giant;   140
Anyway, I can say he was the mightiest of men
And, astride his horse,* a handsome knight as well.
But if he was broad of back and chest
His build, mid-body, was elegantly slender,
His face befitting his form, his bold lineaments

[7]

cut clean.
But the hue of his every feature
Stunned them: as could be seen,
Not only was this creature
Colossal, he was bright green—   150

Green all over, the man and his garments as well!*
A surcoat snugged him tight at the waist
And, over that, a tunic, closely trimmed inside
With fine fur, the cloth resplendent and furnished
With borders of bright ermine; the hood, turned back,
Looped from his coat-collar and was also lipped with fur.
Neat stockings, tightly drawn up, clung to his calves,
All green, and green also the spurs that hung below,
And they glinted gold against the striped silk hose
Of his stockinged feet* fixed in the stirrups.   160
And all his garments this unearthly green
Down to the bars of his belt, and the shining stones
That richly studded the magnificent array
Around the saddle, and around himself: a silken ground
The details of whose embroidery would be difficult
To describe, with its delicate birds and butterflies
In bright green, and a hem of hammered gold;
The cords of the breast-harness, the beautiful crupper-cloth,
The burnished bridle-stud of baked enamel,
Even the steel of the stirrups on which he stood,   170
The saddle-bows and the broad saddle-skirts—
All glinted with the greenish glow of jewels;
And the steed he rode of the same bright
         green strain:
    A horse of massive limbs,

[8]

Most difficult to restrain;
A useful mount!—with gems
Studding his bridle and rein.

And he was fresh-looking, this fellow decked out green.
The hair of his head matched his horse's coat: 180
Bright hair, curling and cascading down his back;
And, bunched on his chest, a bushy beard
Which, with the locks that hung from his head,
Was well-trimmed just above the elbow-joints
So half his arms were hidden beneath hair
Which cleaved to his neck like a king's cape.*
The horse's mane was like that mantle of hair,
Groomed and combed, and neatly knotted,
Plaited and filigreed in gold and green—
One hank of hair to each strand of gold.   190
The tail and the forelock were alike in detail;
The bright green bands around them both
Were strung all along with studded stones
And knit together with a knotted thong
Along which a row of bells rang brilliantly.
No one watching had ever before beheld
A horse like that—and such a horseman had never crossed
        their tracks:
    To them he looked as bright
    As summer lightning that cracks   200
    The sky, and no man might
    Withstand his dreadful axe.

And yet he wore no hauberk, bore no helm,
No mail or metal-plate—no arms or armour at all:

[9]

No spear to thrust, no shield against the shock of battle,
But in one hand a solitary branch of holly
That shows greenest when all the groves are leafless;*
In the other hand he grasped his axe—a huge thing,
A dreadful weapon, difficult to describe:
The head of the big blade over a yard in length,   210
The spike of green steel and wrought gold,
The blade brightly polished, with a broad edge
Beautifully cast to bite keen as a razor;
The shaft he grimly gripped it by, a straight staff
Wound with iron bands right to the end,
Engraved all about with elegant green designs,
Circled with lace-work lashed to the end
And looped round and round the long handle
With plenty of priceless tassels, attached
With bright green buttons, richly braided.   220
And now he shoves past them all, heaves into the hall
And rides right up to the High Table, afraid
Of nothing. He greeted no one, just glared over their heads.
The first words he spoke were these: 'Where is', he said,
'The leader of this lot?* I'd be pleased indeed
If he came forward and traded a few words
        with me.'
    He looked at every knight,
    Strutted, and rolled his eye;
    Stopped, fixed them in his sight   230
    To find whose fame stood high.

And they gazed at him a long moment, amazed.
Everyone wondered what it might mean
That a man and his mount could both be coloured

The green of sprouting grass, and even greener—
Like emerald enamel that glowed on a ground of gold.
They studied him, waited, stalked up warily, stood
Wondering what in the world the man might do.
They'd seen strange things, but never a sight like this;
They thought it must be a sort of magic, or a dream.   240
Most of the men were too terrified to reply;
Struck dumb by his words, they waited, stock-still.
A pall of torpor settled over the hall
As if all dozed. Their talk dropped and their tongues
             went dry,
      Not only, I think, from fear,
      But also from courtesy,
      To give the king they revere
      Chance of a first reply.

The king, from the high board, beholds these curious things,   250
Then, quite free of fear, greets him graciously.
He says: 'Well, sir, you're surely welcome here.
I am the master of this hall and my name is Arthur.
Do dismount and bide with us a while—
Whatever your wish, we'll learn about it later.'
'No, so help me, He that reigns in Heaven!
To pass time in this place was not my plan at all.
But because your name, my lord, is so renowned—
Your castle and your court—and your knights known
As the hardiest on horseback, in armour the most   260
Formidable, the fiercest at mêlées and tournaments,
The bravest and best in the wide world,
And because they say the bright crown of courtesy
Itself sits here—these things have brought me by,

Nothing but these for, as sure as I bear this branch,
I travel in peace and seek no trouble.
Had I come belligerently, were I bent on war,
I have a hauberk at home, and a helm also,
A shield and a sharp spear, both shining bright;
And I have other weapons to wield, that's for certain.   270
But, since I want no war, my dress is innocent.
So, if you're as bold as everybody says,
You'll grant me graciously the sport that I seek
            by right.'
        'Well, if you're hungering,
        Sir knight, sir courteous knight,
        To try your strength,' said the king,
        'You'll certainly have your fight.'

'No, no, I'm not brewing for trouble, I tell you—besides,
It's clear there's no one here but beardless boys.   280
If I bore armour, if I sat on a battle-steed,
No man could match me among these milk-sops.
I need only some diversion for the new season.
It's Yuletide and New Year. Here are many young men.
If any now hold himself bold enough,
If any so hot-blooded or so hare-brained,
Has the stomach to strike one stroke for another,*
I'll give him the gift of this beautiful battle-axe
Which weighs heavy enough for his every wish.
And I shall bear the first blow, as I am, bare-necked.   290
Now, if any man has the mettle to meet my challenge
Let him step down and seize this weapon.
There, I throw it down, let him take it as his own.
I'll receive the first blow right here, without blenching,

[12]

If he but allow me to return that blow however
      I may;
   And yet I'll give him respite:
   A whole year, plus a day—
   So, if your liver's not white,
   Quick now, who's ready to say?'   300

If they were astounded at first, the crowd in the court
Went even quieter now, both high and low.
The horseman swivelled himself about in the saddle
And rolled his red eyes around, most horribly,
Bunched together his brows of bristling green,
Wagged his beard this way and that, and watched.
When no word came he gave a great hacking cough,
Carked his throat clear, most eloquently, and spoke:
'And this is supposed to be Arthur's house,' he cried,
'Whose fame flies through the remotest regions!*   310
Where are your boasts of valour now, your bold victories,
Your pride, your prizes, your wrath and rousing words?
Am I right? All the pageantry and power of the Round Table
Made nothing by the words of one man?
You're all white with fear, and not a whack fallen!'
And he laughed so loud the king blanched with anger,
Then his brow darkened in shame, his face flushed
      blood-dim—
   He grew as wild as the wind;
   The whole hall turned grim.   320
   Then, being of noble kind,
   The king strode up to him

And replied: 'By Heaven, sir, your request's very silly,

But as you ask for a silly thing I'll see you have it.
No man here is scared by what you've said.
Give me your great battle-axe, in the name of God.
I'll easily provide what you've pleaded for!'
He leaps down lightly, seizes the man's hand
Who also dismounts in high disdain.
Arthur takes the axe. He grips the huge handle,   330
And swings it, practising to hack him down.
The fellow pulls himself up to his full height,
Taller than any man in the hall by a head and more.
He stands there, looking serious, smoothing his beard—
Remote, expressionless. He draws his coat down,
Unafraid, no more dismayed by the thought of an axe-blow
Than if a knight nearby had fetched him a flagon
              of wine.
       Beside the queen, Gawain
       Bows to the king, gives sign: 340
       'Please, my good liege, it's plain
       This little fight is mine.

I would ask you,' continued Gawain, to his master and king,
'To bid me rise from my bench and stand beside you,
So that I can quit the table courteously
Without causing displeasure to my lady queen.
I wish to give counsel before this wise court
For, truth to tell, it does not appear proper to me
That a demand like this, delivered with such disdain,
Should be dealt with—whether you wish or no—directly,   350
By you alone, while all around you sit many men
Than whom few under heaven are firmer in will
Or stronger in body when a battle begins.

[14]

I am the weakest and the least in wit;
Loss of my life is therefore of little account.
I am, by birth, your nephew; besides that, nothing.
My one virtue, your blood that runs in my veins.
Since this affair's so foolish and unfit for you
And since I asked soonest, please leave it to me.
If I have blundered, let the whole hall, without blame,   360
       decree.'*

     The nobles thereupon
     Confer, and all agree:
     Gawain should take him on,
     And let the king stay free.

Then the king commanded the knight to stand
And he rose up promptly, prepared himself correctly,
Knelt down before the king and felt the cold weapon;
And the king graciously gave it him, held up his hand
And granted him God's blessing, commended him, praying   370
That his heart and his hand remain resolute:
'Take care, cousin,' said the king, 'how you swing at him,
For, if you strike him right, I'm really sure
You'll withstand any blow he plans to give you back.'
Gawain, axe in hand, goes towards the man
Who bravely waits for him, afraid not a whit.
Then the green knight speaks to sir Gawain:
'Let's repeat our agreement before we go further,*
But first I entreat you, sir, teach me
Your true name, that I may trust you.'*   380
'In good faith,' said the good knight, 'I am called Gawain,
And I am to make this cut at you, come what may,
And a twelvemonth from now I'll take another one

[15]

From you, with whatever weapon you choose, to pay
      it back.'
    The knight gives him reply:
    'Ah, sir Gawain—what luck!
    I am pleased exceedingly
    That you will make the stroke.

'Yes, by Heaven, sir Gawain,' the knight says,   390
'I'm delighted I'll get this gift from your hand.
You have repeated precisely and truthfully
All the conditions of the covenant I asked of the king,
Save that you will assure me by your troth,
You will seek me yourself, wherever your search
Takes you in the world—and you'll win the same wages
As you give me before this fine company.'
'Where shall I find you, sir, where are you from?
By Him that made me, I know nothing of your home;
Neither do I know you, your court, or what you're called—   400
Nothing. So please tell me now your name
And I'll use all my wits to find my way to you:
I swear by that, and there's *my* troth on it.'
'Enough for New Year's Day, no more needs saying,'
Continued the man in green to the courteous Gawain.
'You'll not discover that until you've dealt your blow.
When you have struck properly then I'll provide you with
All you need know about my castle and name.
Only then need you learn where I live, to keep the contract.
And if I keep quiet the bargain's even better: 410
You can remain here, all year, in your own country!
        Enough said!
    Now grip this axe until

[16]

We see of what stuff you're made.'
'Gladly, sir, that I will!'
Says Gawain. He strokes the blade.

On the ground the green knight girds himself;
He lets his head fall forward, revealing the flesh.
His long locks tumble down over his crown
Baring the nape of his neck for the blow.   420
Gawain sets his left foot slightly forward;
He grips the axe and lifts it over his head
Then brings it down, neat and quick, on the bare nape
So that the sharp blade shattered the neck-bone,
Bit through the flesh and sliced the knight in two.
The flashing blade bit a deep groove in the ground,
The head sprang from the body and hurtled to earth
And some fumbled it with their feet as it rolled around.
Blood spurted from the great body and splattered the green,
But still he didn't fall, didn't falter at all,   430
But strode forward steadily on firm thighs,
Reached out fiercely among the ranks of knights,
Gripped his handsome head and quickly picked it up;
Then hurried to his horse, caught hold of the halter
Stepped into the stirrups and swung up,
Holding his head, by its own hair, in his hand,
Then sat there in the saddle, stubbornly,
As if nothing had happened—though now he was wearing
            no head.
        He twisted around. Amazed   440
        At that gross trunk that bled,
        In pure terror they gazed,
        And marvelled at what he said,

[17]

For now he holds the head in his hand up high
And turns it to face the noblest at the table.*
It lifts its eyelids, gives them a long stare, then
Slowly opens its mouth, and these words come out:
'Be prepared to do as you promised, Gawain;
Seek me faithfully until you find me, sir.
As you have pledged in the presence of these noble knights,   450
You will go to the Green Chapel, to receive
Such a blow as you have dealt—you now deserve it!—
That blow to be borne on New Year's morning.
Men know me as the knight of the Green Chapel,
And, if you ask, you cannot fail to find me.
Come, therefore—or be known as a craven coward!'*
With a quick twist he tugs at the reins
And, still holding his head, rides through the hall doorway.
His horse's hooves kick fire from the flint-stone.
Which way he was headed no one could readily say,   460
Nor could they name the country whence he came.

      And so?
   Well, the king and his chosen knight
   Laughed as they watched him go*—
   Yet they had to admit
   They'd seen a marvel too.

Though Arthur's heart stood still in wonder,
He showed no sign of it, but said aloud
To his queen, in his most courteous manner,
'Dear lady, please don't be dismayed.   470
Such deeds are welcome at the Christmas season,
Like the interludes,* the laughing and singing
And the carol-rounds with royal lords and ladies.

Nevertheless, now I may proceed with my meal
For I have seen a marvel, I mustn't deny it.'
He caught Gawain's eye, and lightly said to his knight:
'Now sir, hang up your axe,* it's hacked enough for today.'
And they hung it high on a drape over the dais,
That men might gaze upon it as a marvel
And point to it, and tell the tale of its power.   480
Then they went together to the table,
The king and his knight, who were now served in splendour,
With double helpings of the daintiest things:
All kinds of fine fare, and more music.
So they passed their time in delight, until at last
      night fell.
   Now, Gawain, think of your quest,
   And let no terror quell
   Your courage in the test
   You have taken on. Think well!   490

II

THIS novel event was Arthur's New Year present
At the dawn of the year; he yearned for such adventures.
Yet they all wanted for words as they went to their tables,
For now the business in hand is heavy, burdensome.
Gawain was glad to begin the sport in the hall
But, if the game grew serious, think it no surprise,
For if men are feather-wits when the wine's flowing,
Time races on, nothing remains unchanged;
Our endings rarely square with our beginnings.*
Yuletide once past, the year followed fast behind;*   500
Each new season turning in its time:
After Christmas, the crabbed fasting-time of Lent
When people eat fish for meat, and simple fare.*
Then the world's fresh weather fights with winter:
Cold shrinks into the ground, clouds rise;
Warm rain shuttles down in flashing showers
Over the flatlands; flowers poke up,
Fields and groves put on their freshest green;
Birds start building, they call out loudly
For the calm of summer that spreads its balm on valleys   510
        and slopes.
    Rich hawthorn-blossoms swell
    And burst in rows; in the copse
    New bird-sounds run, pell-mell,
    Through the glorious full tree-tops.

And then broad summer, when balmy winds

Out of the west breathe on bush and seed,
And plants under a wide sky dance in joy;
When dew gathers and slips in drops from wet leaves
As they bask in the sumptuous beams of the bright sun.   520
Then autumn, with sombre shadows striding towards
Winter, warning the grain to grow to fullness.
On dry days he drives the rising dust
Up from the folding fields, where it spirals high.
In the huge heavens, winds wrestle with the sun;
Tawny leaves are ripped from the linden tree
And lush grass in the field leans over, and greys.
Whatever rose up earlier now ripens and rots;
The year dwindles, all days seem yesterdays.
Winter winds on as it will, as it has done   530
          of old.
     And when the Michaelmas moon*
     Burns on the icy wold
     Gawain fears he must soon
     Make his quest through the cold.

Till All Hallows' Day he stays with Arthur
Who, on that holiday, held a feast in his homage
With much revelry and rejoicing of the Round Table.
The lords, out of courtesy, with their comely ladies,
Came in sorrow for love of the young knight,   540
And yet, though sad, they still made jests,
Not showing their feelings but suppressing their sorrow.
After the meal, in gloomy mood, Gawain came to the king
Concerning his journey, and said straight out:
'It is time, my lord, to take my leave of you.
You know what it's about, and I'll not bother you

With all my difficulties, and the small details.
I'm duty bound to depart tomorrow, without delay,
To get my blow from the man in green, as God decrees.'
Then the best men of the court gathered together: 550
Iwain and Erik, and many more besides;
Sir Doddinvale de Savage, the Duke of Clarence,
Lancelot, Lionel, that good man, Lucan;
Sir Bors, Sir Bedevere, big men both,
Mador de la Port,* and also many more
Of great renown. They gathered around the king.
Now, heavy with care, they counselled the knight
And many suffered their sorrow secretly,
Regretting that the good Gawain should make the quest
And bear such a horrible blow, and not hit back,   560
       but wait.
    Gawain put on good cheer.
    'Why should I hesitate?'
    He said. 'Kind or severe,
    We must engage our fate.'*

He stays on all that day. Next dawn he dresses,
Calls early for his arms,* they are duly carried in.
First, a red silk carpet is spread on the floor
And the lustrous gilt armour laid on it, glistening.
Dressed in a doublet of worked silk from Turkestan   570
And a king's cape, cleverly made, closed at the neck,
Its inside hems fringed with shining fur,
He strolls among the armour and strokes the steel.
They fix steel sabatons onto his feet,
Lap his legs in gleaming metal greaves,
Their brilliant knee-joints newly burnished,

And fasten them, with knotted filigree, to his knees.
Fine thigh-pieces, lashed with leather thongs,
Cover his thick thighs, and close over them.
A coat of link-mail, its rings glinting,   580
Clasps him round, over a tunic of finest cloth;
Polished arm-pieces, with gay-coloured elbow-guards,
Are fastened to his arms and, last, gauntlets of steel.
In all, the finest-fitting gear to guard him on
       his ride:
    His coat-armour, trimmed by hand,
    His gold spurs proudly tied;
    Girt with a silken band,*
    His broadsword swung at his side.

Buckled up, the knight glowed in his bright armour;   590
The smallest lace or loop gleamed gold.
Clothed in this manner, he goes to hear Mass*
Solemnly celebrated at the great altar.
Then he comes to the king, and his court-companions,
Takes his leave courteously of the lords and ladies;
Escorting him out, they kissed him, commending him to
  Christ.
By then Gringolet* stood ready, girt with a saddle
That, studded with new nails cut specially
And bordered with gold, gleamed brightly.
The bridle was richly barred and wrapped with gold.   600
The furnishings of the breast-harness, of the fine skirts,
Crupper and caparison, matched those of the saddle-bows,
And all was gilded with new gold nails
That flickered and flashed like tiny sun-flares.
He takes hold of the helm, which is strongly stapled

And thickly padded inside, and quickly kisses it.*
It sat high on his head, held with a hasp
Behind, and a bright strap clasping the visor
Embroidered and set with the best gems
On a broad silk hem, with birds on the seams: 610
Parrots preening their wings, depicted among
Turtle-doves, and true-love knots, so numerous
It must have taken the ladies seven seasons
        to sew.
     The circlet round his crown
     Was even more precious, though;
     Its device of diamond-stone,
     Burned with a dusky glow.

THEN they show him the shield, its gules shimmering,
And its pentangle* picked out in pure gold.   620
He grips the girdle of the shield, flicks it quickly
Round his neck. It fits him neatly.
Now, though it delay me, I propose to say
Why the pentangle bedecks the noble knight:
It is a design that Solomon devised,* a sign
And token of truth*—quite rightly too,
For its figure comprises five points
And its lines overlap and link with each other
With no ending anywhere; and men in England
Call it, accordingly, the Knot without End.   630
Therefore it suits the knight in his bright armour
Ever faithful, five times, five ways in each.
Gawain was known as a good knight, like gold
Purified of fault, his virtues clearly and openly
        revealed.

[24]

The pentangle he was wearing
On surcoat and on shield
Bespoke his gentle bearing
And trust that would not yield.

First, he was found without fault in his five senses;* 640
Again, his five fingers never failed him,
And all his faith in the world was in the five wounds
That Christ received on the Cross, as the Creed tells;*
And whenever this warrior was embroiled in battle
His sole and steadfast thought was simply that
His courage came, finally, from the five joys
The courteous Queen of Heaven had from her child;*
Therefore, painted in comely colours, he carried
Her gracious image; it glowed inside his shield
And when he gazed thereon his courage never wavered. 650
Of the fifth group of five he honoured constantly
The first four were generosity, good fellowship,
Cleanness, and courtesy, uncurbed and unimpaired;
Lastly, compassion,* surpassing all: these final five,
More firmly fixed on that knight than on any other,
These five, compounded by faith, conjoined in him,
Each one woven with the other, each one unending,
Fastened on five points that never faltered,
Nor strayed from each other, but stayed together
Always without end, as I have found, no matter where 660
A man might begin the design, or strive to close it.
Therefore the knot on this new shield was fashioned
Royally, in red gold on red gules:*
Such is the pure pentangle which people of old
were taught.

He is ready now in his gay
Armour; his lance is brought.
He took it, gave them good-day—
For evermore, he thought.

He jabbed the steed with his spurs and sped away   670
So fast that sparks flew from the flint-stone.
At the sight of the knight riding off, they sighed.
Grieving for Gawain, all the lords and ladies
Said truthfully to each other: 'By heaven, it's a pity
That he is gone, with his huge gift for life!
To find his equal will be far from easy.
It would have been wiser to proceed discreetly,
To have endowed the noble knight with a dukedom.
He would have been a lord of men, a magnificent leader;
A much better destiny than being destroyed, his head   680
Struck off by an elfish man out of selfish pride.
Whoever heard of a king heeding the counsel
Of capricious knights in the nonsense of Christmas games?'
Much warm water flowed from their eyes
When the good man went from their dwelling
        that day.
    He bade them well, then took
    Himself, without delay—
    As I heard tell from the book—
    Along his tortuous way.   690

Now the knight rides through the realm of Logres:*
Sir Gawain, in God's service, finding it no game.
At times, companionless, he takes his rest at night
Where he finds little of the food to his liking.

[26]

No good friend but his horse in those woods and hills,
And no one save God to speak to on his way,
While he is nearing the wastes of Northern Wales.
He keeps to the right of the Isles of Anglesey,
Fords the foreshore by the promontory, first
Wading over at Holyhead, then heaving ashore once more   700
Into the forest of Wirral,* the wilderness. Few there
Were loved by God or men of goodwill.
And wherever he went, asking those whom he met
If they knew anything of a knight in green
Or by chance, of the Green Chapel in the region around,
They said, no, no, they'd never seen him,
Nor even heard of a man in that land, dressed all
      in green.
    He turns down dreary ways
    Where dark hillsides lean,   710
    His mood changing as the day's,
    But the chapel could not be seen.

He clambers over rough slopes in curious regions;
Estranged from his friends, he rides on, ranging far.
At each water-ford, or river-reach that he crossed
He found, more often than not, a foe before him—
One so foul and violent he had to fight him.
Among those hills he met so many marvels
It's hard to tell a tenth part of them all.
Sometimes he wars with dragons, or with wolves;   720
With wodwos, who watched him from woodland crags;
With bulls and bears; sometimes with savage boars,
And giants from the high fells,* who followed him.
Had he not been brave and sturdy, not served God,

He would have died, been destroyed many times.
But if those fights were fierce, winter was worse,
When chilling water spilled out of the clouds
Freezing as it fell, pelting the pale ground.
Almost killed by sleet, he sleeps in all his armour
More nights than enough among the rough rocks,   730
Where plummeting cascades from the summits ran cold
Or hung over his head in hard ice-blades.
This way, in danger, in pain and hardship,
Over the land the knight rides till Christmas Eve,
      alone;
    Then, in despair on his ride,
    He cries in a plangent tone
    That Mary be his guide
    To a house, a warm hearth-stone.

Through the morning he rides on merrily,* beside a hill,   740
Into a dark wood, wonderfully wild.
High hills all around; below, a grove of oaks,
Huge and hoary, more than a hundred of them.
Hazel and hawthorn were tangled together there,
And everywhere rough mounds of hairy moss.
Hunched on bare branches, doleful birds
Piped out pitiful calls in the bitter cold.
The knight glides under them on Gringolet
Through bogs and quagmires, quite alone,
Fearing the whims of fate, worried that he would   750
Never see the Lord's service, Who, on that same night,
Was born of a maid to assuage our sorrow.*
And he implored Him, saying, 'I beseech thee, Lord,
And Mary, mild Mother, so dear to us,

That I might soon hear mass in a holy place
And Matins in the morning—I ask it meekly,
And therefore promptly say my **Paternoster**, **Ave**
   and **Creed**.'*
  And, riding as he prayed,
  He repented each misdeed,   760
  And signed himself, and said:
  'May Christ's Cross lend me speed!'

Hᴀʀᴅʟʏ had he made the sign three times
When, in the midst of the wood, he saw a moated castle
On open ground, rising from a mound; boughs
Of massive trees by the moats enclosed it.
Built on meadow-ground, with a beautiful park all round,
It was the finest castle ever kept by a knight.
A spiked palisade, its palings tight together,
Surrounded many trees, and ran two miles around.   770
The knight studied the stronghold from the side
As it glimmered and glowed among the tall oak trees.
He removed his helm in reverence, humbly thanked
Both Jesus and Saint Julian* for their bounteous deed
And their great courtesy in granting him his plea.
'Now, grant me a good night's lodging,' he beseeched.
Then, with his gold spurs, he urged Gringolet on.
By good chance he had chosen the main road
And it brought him to the drawbridge quick
   and straight.   780
  The bridge was drawn upright
  And shut tight every gate;
  Against the wind's worst might
  Those walls were inviolate.

The horseman waited at the bank, hesitated at the brink
Of the double ditch* that ran around the castle.
The walls sank down far into the dark water,
And rose to a huge height over it;
The fine stone soared up to the cornices.
Its battlements were formed in a style most fitting,   790
With graceful turrets spaced out at intervals
And a row of lovely loopholes with locking shutters.
A better barbican the knight had never seen.
Further in, he descried the wall of the high hall
With its bold, regular towers and tough battlements
And clusters of painted pinnacles, cleverly joined,
Their high carved tops far up in the sky.
He also caught sight of the chalk-white chimneys
That shimmered immaculately on the tower-tops:
From any vantage-point so many turrets and towers   800
Amid the parapets, and scattered so thickly,
It seemed a pure fancy, or a model made from paper.*
From his horse, the knight thought it so inviting
He wondered: 'If I can work my way inside,
A respite here in the Holy Season would be a time
            of grace.'
        He called out. After a time,
        A porter, high up, whose face
        Smiled down, acknowledged him
        And welcomed him to that place.   810

'Good sir,' said Gawain, 'would you take a message for me
To the lord of the castle, and ask for lodging?'
'Yes, by Saint Peter, though I'd guess', replied the porter,*
'You're welcome to lodge here as long as you like.'

[30]

He hurried off, and straightway came back
With many more people, to receive the knight properly.*
They let fall the drawbridge, walked out towards him
And knelt down in courtesy on the cold ground
To greet the man in a manner they gauged befitting.
They let him ride through the great gates, now wide   820
Apart. He bade them stand, passed over the bridge
Where several of the men steadied his saddle.
He dismounted, and more men stabled his steed.
And then the knights and their squires descended
To greet him, and lead him off to the lord's hall.
As he unhasped his helmet, everyone hurried
To seize it in their hands, and serve this noble man.
They relieved him of sword and shield and bore them off.
Then, courteously, he greeted each man among them.
They all pressed forward proudly to honour the prince   830
And brought him to the hall, still in his bright armour
Where a fire burned fiercely in the big grate.
Then the lord of the castle came forth from his chamber
To greet with high honour the man in his hall.
He said: 'You may stay as long as you like.
All here in this hall is yours, to do whatever you have
           in mind.'
       'My warmest thanks!' They embrace
       Gladly, their arms entwined.
       'May Christ reward your grace;   840
       You are indeed most kind.'

Gawain gazed at the man that greeted him,
And a powerful prince he looked, the castle's lord:
A towering fellow, trim, and in his prime.

[31]

His wide beard glistened like a beaver's hide.
Stern-looking, on stalwart legs he strode forward,
Fiery-faced, his eye fierce, and his speech
Noble, an excellent thing, the knight thought,
For him to be master of the men of that castle.
The lord turned towards a side-room, straightway ordered   850
That a servant be given to Gawain, to tend him.
In a trice, at his call, many came and took him
To a bright room with regal bedding:
Curtains of silk cloth with gilded hems,
Delicate coverlets of lovely smooth sable,
With parti-coloured panels and stitch-worked seams,
And the curtains ran along cords of red-gold rings.
Silks of Toulouse and Turkestan spread down the walls
And fine carpets, matching them, covered the floor.*
And there, with merry quips, they quickly removed,   860
To his great relief, his mail and gleaming raiments,
And promptly fetched him fine fresh robes
To choose from and change into, as he wished.
No sooner had he chosen one with flowing skirts
That suited him, and put it on, than it seemed to everyone
By his appearance that spring was clearly beginning
For its glorious colours, as it lightly covered his limbs,
Caught fire and glowed and, surely, they thought,
Christ had never created a creature like
              this knight.   870
        They saw, no matter where
        He came from, this man might
        Be a prince without any peer
        Wherever bold men fight.

A seat with sumptuous furnishings, its cover-cloths
And quilted cushions crafted masterfully,
Was fetched and set before the fire where
The coals glowed. A glorious cloak of brilliant silk,
Opulently appointed, was placed over his shoulders.
It was fringed inside with the finest animal-fur,   880
Earth's best ermine, the broad hood also of fur.
He sat there, looking most handsome in that seat.
Warmth ran through his limbs and his liveliness
Returned. Soon they set up a trestle-table
Laid with a new cloth and napkins, spotless white,
A salt-cellar, and cutlery, all silver.
He washed in his good time, and went to his food.
Serving-men, with becoming grace, brought bowls
Of several excellent soups, exquisitely seasoned,
Steaming and brimming over, then dishes of various fish:*   890
Some baked in bread, some broiled on the embers,
Some boiled, or stewed with spices, in their juice,
All served with delicate sauces that he relished.
And he politely proclaimed it a feast, again
And again, whereon they bade him, again and again,
      'Please eat!
   This fast is for your good;
   Tomorrow's fare will be meat.'
   Gawain was in jovial mood,
   Flushed with the wine and heat.   900

Then they asked, and ascertained in a tactful way,
By detailed questions put to the knight discreetly,
That he was of Arthur's court; and he courteously revealed
That he was a knight and kinsman of King Arthur,

[33]

That royal and renowned lord of the Round Table;
That it was, in fact, Gawain who sat before them,
And he'd arrived, as chance decided, at Christmastide.
When the lord learned that Gawain was staying with him
He laughed loudly, delighted with his luck.
And all the folk in the hall were full of joy   910
And presented themselves without ado because all virtue,
Excellence, strengh and good breeding belonged
To this reputable person, praised everywhere,
Whose honour was held highest before all men.
And each man said quietly to his companion:
'Now we shall see a marvellous show of manners,
And learn from the intricate turns of his conversation;
Without even seeking we'll see just what
Good talk can be, for the prince of courtesy walks
Among us. Surely God has showered his grace   920
On us in granting us a guest such as Gawain
At the season when all on earth sing the birth of God
              above!
        Surely we shall receive
        From him a knowledge of
        Fine ways and, I believe,
        The subtle speech of love.'*

By that time dinner was done. The fine company
Rose. Night was now closing in.
Chaplains made their way to the chapel   930
And bells rang out richly, as befitting
The blessed evensong of the festive season.
The lord attends; his lady is there also.
She goes in gracefully, to her private pew

[34]

And straightway Gawain enters the chape...
The lord takes hold of a fold of his gown an...
To a seat, acknowledges him, speaks his nam...
Adding, moreover, that his presence gladdens...
Than anything. Gawain thanks him again. The...
Then sit together silently through the service.
Later, the lady wished to look on the knight:
She came from her pew, accompanied by peerless ...men,
But she, in looks and complexion, the loveliest of all:
Well-groomed, graceful, perfectly poised—
Even lovelier than Guinevere, thought Gawain.
He goes forth into the chancel, to greet her formally.
Another lady led her by the left hand,
An elderly lady, one clearly much older than her,
Who was held in high honour by everyone there.
These two were quite unlike in every way: 950
One was winsome and young, the other withered.
A glow of roseate colour shone on the first,
While rough and wrinkled cheeks hung from the other.
Kerchiefs and clusters of pearls adorned the younger;
Her breast and bright throat, showing bare,
Glowed more freshly than the first snow on the hills.
The other, swathed in a gorget that hid her neck,
Her swart chin wrapped in chalk-white veils,
Her forehead muffled up in folds of silk,
Was trellised round with trefoils and jingling rings,   960
And nothing of her uncovered but her black brows,
Her two eyes, her nose and naked lips—
All sour to the sight, all strangely bleared:
A beautiful lady, by God, let it not be
      denied!

[35]

body, and thick waist,
Her buttocks full and wide;*
Much daintier, to his taste,
The young one at her side.

Gawain, gazing on the one who looked so gracious,   970
Received the lord's consent to go forward in greeting.
He faces the old one first, bows very low;
The fairer one, very lightly, he embraces
In comely fashion, kisses her, speaks to her courteously.
They beg his acquaintance; he eagerly requests,
In all solicitude, to be their true servant.
They take him between them and, talking, lead him
To a side-room where first of all, they call
For spices,* which men speed to bring them unstintingly,
With beakers of warming wine at each return.   980
The jubilant lord leapt about in joy
Telling them, time and again, to amuse themselves.
He snatched his hood off,* gaily snared it on a spear
Declaring 'He wins the honour of wearing this
Who makes up the most amusing Christmas game—
And, by my faith, with the help of my friends, I'll fight
The best of you before I give this garment up.'
With whirling words and laughter the lord enjoys himself
That night, with many games for sir Gawain, to make
      him glad,   990
    Until, the hour being late,
    'Bring lights!' the fine host said.
    Gawain gave all goodnight
    And went off to his bed.

So the morning when men are mindful of the time
When the Lord, for our destiny, was born to die,
For whose sake joy wakens in every house in the world,
Fell to them there as well that day: delicious foods,
Both at the formal dinner and the more casual meals,
Were plentifully served, by strong men at the long dais.   1000
The ancient lady sat in the loftiest place
With the lord, I believe out of courtesy, beside her.
Gawain and the lovelier lady sat together
At the central board where the food was served first.
Then all in the hall were subsequently served
According to their state—the appropriate form.
There was meat, great mirth and much delight,
Difficult indeed to describe to you now
If I tried to tell it in all its finer details.
But I do know that Gawain and the lovely lady   1010
Delighted in each other's bright company,
And in the deft dalliance of courtly conversation.
No innuendo darkened their delicate speech;
Their witty word-play surpassed the sports of the other lords.
        With blares
    Of trumpets, drums' loud measures
    And pipes with their pleasing airs,
    All tended to their pleasures
    As these two looked to theirs.

Great mirth and merriment that day and the next,   1020
And the third, as pleasure-filled, followed hard.
They celebrated St John's day* with joy and jubilation.
This was the final festive day for in the grey
Of morning they knew many guests were going.

[37]

So they whiled away the night in high style,
Drinking wine and dancing the finest carols.
At last, very late, all who were not of that place,
All those who were going, slowly took their leave.
Gawain gave them farewell. The lord leads him aside,
Brings him to his own bedroom, beside the fire;   1030
There he detains him, shows his delight, thanks him
For the high honour he has heaped on them all
In staying at his house for that solemn season,
And in gracing his court with his gay company:
'Indeed, as long as I live, I'll be the better for it,
That Gawain has been my guest at God's feast.'
'My thanks are to you,' says Gawain, 'for in good faith,
I claim the honour as mine, may the High King reward you.
I am most eager to please you, to perform your every wish,
Both small and great, as I am bound by my knight's   1040
          decree.'
          The lord tries hard to hold
          Gawain in his company
          Much longer, but he is told
          By the knight it cannot be.

Then he put many questions to his guest, courteously
Asked him what grim business forced him at that time
To ride so resolutely from the king's court alone,
Even before the end of the festive season.
'Indeed, sir,' said Gawain, 'your question comes home.   1050
A difficult and urgent duty spurred me on:
I am summoned to seek a particular place
Of whose location I have no notion at all.
And I must not miss it on New Year's morning

[38]

For all the rich land in the realm of Logres.
My lord, please let me put you a question:
Tell me truthfully if you've heard any man mention
The Green Chapel, or the ground that church stands on,
Or the knight who keeps it, clothed in bright green.
A meeting with that man at such a landmark,   1060
If I'm still alive, was set by solemn agreement,
And there's but little time till the New Year.
If God permit, I would set my gaze on him
More willingly, by God's Son, than I would on anything
In the world. So, by your leave, I'm bound to proceed;
There are barely three days more. I must make ready
For I'd rather meet quick death than defeat in my quest.'
The lord laughed. 'In that case you can stay,
Because I will show you well before where to go.
Let the whereabouts of the Green Chapel worry you no
          longer.   1070
You can rest at ease, lie in as long as you please
Until late morning on the first day of the year,
Then ride to the meeting place at midday, to do what you
                    must do.
          Stay until New Year's Day,
          Then you can rise, and go.
          We'll set you on your way.
          It's only a mile or so.'

At this, Gawain, most gratified, laughed gladly:
'My heartfelt thanks—indeed, you have helped exceedingly! 1080
My quest is at an end. I shall spend, at your behest,
Therefore, a longer time, and do as you would wish.'
Then the knight took hold of him, sat beside him,

And bade the ladies enter to please them better,
And they passed a delightful time before the fire.
The lord, in his levity, let forth shrieks of glee
Like someone losing his wits, or unaware of his acts,
Calling out to the knight in a loud cry:
'So, you have chosen to do what I asked of you!
Will you promise, here and now, to hold to that vow?'   1090
'Most certainly I will, sir,' said the noble knight,
'While I bide in your house I'm bound by your command.'
'Well, because you've come so far and travelled hard,
Then kept late nights with me, you're not quite rested.
You need nourishment and sleep, that's easily seen.
So remain in your room and rest at your leisure
In the morning, till Mass, then go to your meal
With my wife, as soon as you wish. She will sit
With you for company till I come back to court.

       Understood?   1100
         Quite early I shall rise
         For hunting in the wood.'*
         With this, Gawain complies,
         And bows, as polite men should.

'Furthermore,' said the lord, 'let's settle on a bargain.
Whatever I win at hunting will henceforth be yours;
And you, in turn, will yield whatever you earn.*
There, my fine fellow, swear on it truly,
Whether we win or lose,' demanded the lord.
'By God,' replied Gawain, 'I'm ready for that.   1110
I must say I'm glad you wish to play this game.'
'Bring us all drinks, the bargain's driven!'
Said the lord of the castle. And they laughed delightedly,

And drank wine, chatted, dallied, and delayed,
The lords and ladies, as long as it pleased them to.
Then, with French phrases, and lingering, light douceurs,*
They stayed on even longer, speaking softly,
And kissed each other, and kindly took their leave.
Then their serving-men slowly led them away,
Lighting each to his room with the glow of a bright   1120
       torch-flame.
    But, before bed, their accord
    Again and again they proclaim.
    He knew very well, that lord,
    How to draw out his game.

III

EVEN before daybreak everyone was up.
The guests who were going called their grooms,
And they hurried out to saddle their stout horses,
Get all their gear in order, pack their saddle-pockets.
Guests of the highest rank, dressed ready for riding,   1130
Leapt up lightly, took hold of their bridles,
Each person going where it most pleased him.
The beloved lord of the castle was not the last:
Rigged out for riding, he appeared with his many men.
Straight after Mass he ate a light meal, hastily,*
And hurried to the field, flourishing his bugle.
By the time daylight was gathering over the ground
He and his men were waiting on their huge horses.
His clever huntsmen coupled the hounds in their leashes,
Opened the kennel door and called them forth.   1140
They blew their bugles loudly: three bare notes.
At that, the hounds bayed, making a great furore,
And those that broke away were whipped and turned back.
There were, I'm told, a hundred men of the boldest
            hunting blood.
        The keepers of the hounds
        Took up their posts and stood
        Waiting, while bugle-sounds
        Echoed around the wood.

Creatures in the wild, hearing the hounds, awoke   1150
Trembling; terrified deer raced through the dale.*
They sped away to safer ground, but straightway

[42]

Were blocked by the beaters, with bellows and cries.
They let the high-antlered harts go by
And the big bucks with their huge horn-branches
For the lord had forbidden, in the closed season,
That any man interfere with the male deer.
The hinds were held back with shouts of 'Hey' and 'Hold!'
While the does charged down to the deep dale,
And there you might see men loosing their long   1160
Arrows: at each forest-break the big shafts flew,
Their broad heads biting the tawny hides,
And they cried out, bleeding and dying on the banks,
The hounds racing headlong after the rest.
Hunters, their horns blaring, hurried after:
A mighty cracking sound, as if a cliff were splitting.
Any wild beast beaten back from the high ground,
Who slipped between the bowmen, was driven down
To the stations by the water, and slaughtered there.
The huntsmen who kept those posts were so adept   1170
With their sleek hounds, they quickly stopped them
And, fast as the eye could follow, dragged
       them down.
     The lord galloped, and dismounted,*
     In ecstasy galloped on,
     Riding daylong, undaunted,
     Until the light was gone.

And so the lord enjoys his sport at the forest-border,
And the good man, Gawain, remains in bed,
Lying snug, while the light streams down his walls.*   1180
Under luxurious coverlets, all canopied about,
And drowsing in soft slumber, he dimly hears

[43]

at the threshold. He listens. Now the door
kes his head out of the bed-clothes,
e corner of the curtain, just a little,
ly out to see what it could be.
e lady there, and she is lovely to look upon.
She draws the door close-to behind her, silently,
And moves towards the bed; the man, embarrassed,
Sinks back again soundlessly, feigning sleep.   1190
She steps up lightly, steals towards the bedside,
Brushes back the curtain and cautiously creeps in,
And sits, very softly, on the bed's edge,
Lingering there at leisure to watch him waking.
The lord kept low for a long time also,
Turning over in his mind what this might mean
And what it implied, for it seemed to him a marvel.
But he murmured to himself: 'It would be more seemly
To find out, in the course of conversation, what she wants.'
Soon he woke, and stretched, and turned towards her,   1200
Unlocked his eyelids, and looked surprised,
Then made the sign of the Cross, as if by prayer to escape
          his plight.
          There glowed on her lovely face
          A hue both red and white.
          She seemed the image of grace,
          Her small lips laughing and bright.

'Good morning, sir Gawain,' said the lady merrily.
'What a careless sleeper, to let someone slip in here.
I have trapped you beautifully, unless we strike a bargain   1210
I shall bind you in your bed—of that you can be sure.'
And the lady laughed, made jests and jibes.

[44]

'And a very good morning to you,' said Gawain gaily.
'You may do with me as you wish and I'll be pleased:
In a moment I surrender—and I seek your mercy.
Truly I have no choice, trapped here as I am.'
He jests with her, to joyful peals of merriment.
'But, lovely lady, would you grant me leave
And release your prisoner, prompt him now to rise
That he might slip from his bed to find more fitting clothes?* 1220
Then I'd be more at my ease to talk with you.'
'No, no, my fine sir,' said the sweet lady,
'You shall not budge from your bed. I have another notion.
I shall tuck you up tightly on either side
And then talk with my knight whom I have neatly trapped,
For, yes, I am certain now that you are sir Gawain
Revered by the wide world everywhere you ride.
Your knightly character and courtesy are highly renowned
By all lords and ladies—indeed, by all who live.
And now, you are next to me, and we are alone.   1230
My lord and his loyal men are far away in the forest;
Those in the hall lie sleeping, their ladies also.
The door is shut firm and fastened with a hasp.
And since I have in my house the person whom all prefer
I intend to savour each second: each passing word
        I'll treasure.
    Both my mind and body
    Are only for your pleasure.
    I'm here perforce, and ready
    To serve you at your leisure.'*   1240

'In good faith,' says Gawain, 'that's certainly flattering.
However, I'm not the man whom you have in mind.

[45]

...arly worthy enough, as I well know,
...ire such reverence as you have described.
...uld be happy, by Heaven, if I could please you
...nd be deemed fit, in word and deed, to devote myself
To serving you—a service of purest joy!'
'In good faith, sir Gawain,' said the lady gaily,
'Your excellence exceeds, your powers surpass all others.
To consider them lightly would show little courtesy;   1250
There are many ladies who would love beyond the world
To hold you in their power, as I have you now,
To while away the time with tender words,
To find solace in love, free at last from sorrow:
They would prefer that pleasure to the richest possession.
But praise Him who reigns in Heaven on high,
By whose grace I have wholly in my hand the man desired
          by all.'
      She brought him excellent cheer,
      Being so beautiful,   1260
      And the knight, with tact and care,
      Answered her words in full.

'Mary reward you,* madam,' he said merrily,
'For, truly, I find your kindness most noble.
Most men receive recognition for generous deeds;
The respect I receive is through no merit of mine.
You yourself gain in honouring me this way.'
'Not so,' said the noble lady, 'I know otherwise,
For were I worth all the women who live on earth,
If I held the world's wealth in my very hand,   1270
How could I make a better bargain in a husband?
With the qualities of heart and mind I have come to find

In you—your youth, your grace and gaiety,
Of which I have heard tell, and now know to be true,
There is no man in the world I would choose before you.'
'Beautiful lady, I know you have chosen better;
Yet I am proud of the price you have placed on me.
I shall hold you as my sovereign, serve you steadfastly,
And I shall be your knight, may Christ reward you!'
Thus they discussed many things till mid-morning   1280
And the lady made as if she loved him dearly.
Gawain, more restrained, showed marvellous courtesy.
Were she the brightest beauty, the knight had little love
To spare from his sorrowful quest, which he might not
   forestall.*
  The cut that lays him low
  Assuredly will fall.
  She told him she would go,
  And he agreed withal.

he refuses at first

She said good-bye, laughed, gave a sidelong look;   1290
Then, while she stood there, astonished him with these words:
'May He who rewards fine speeches praise your performance.
However, it's hard to be sure you're really sir Gawain.'*
'Why?' he replied, and quickly questioned her,
Afraid that he may have behaved boorishly.
But the lady blessed him and spoke to him, explaining:
'Gawain is rightly held to be a gracious knight
And courtesy contained in him so completely
He could never dally so long with a lady

coy

Without being moved—if only by some touch or trifle   1300
At a speech's end—out of kindness, to beseech a kiss.'
Gawain said: 'Well, best let it be as you wish:

[47]

s at your command, as becomes a knight,
more: I'll not displease you, no need to plead further.'
ne comes nearer at that, catches him in her arms,
Leans down lovingly and kisses the lord.
They commend each other becomingly to Christ
And she goes out gracefully without more ado.
With that, rather hurriedly, he prepares to rise,
Calls to his chamberlain,* chooses his clothes.   1310
Once ready, he leaves his room and repairs to Mass,
Then to his meal, which the men had made for him.
All that day he made merry, until the rise
       of the moon.
    Never so graciously,
    By the young one and the crone,
    Was knight received. All three
    Enjoyed themselves as one.

And all the while the lord is at his sport
Hunting the barren hinds in wood and heath.   1320
By sundown, he has slain so many beasts—
Does and other deer—it is a marvel to recall.
Then at last all the men-folk flocked together
And deftly built a small hill of the deer they'd killed.
Those of noblest rank went up with their retinue
And chose all those they liked with the choicest fat
And ordered them neatly cut up, as custom demands.*
They strolled around studying them, and found
Two finger-widths of fat on even the worst of them.
They slit open their slots, seized the first stomach,   1330
Cut it out with a keen knife and knit it up.
Next they lopped off the legs, peeled back the pelt,

[48]

Tore the belly open, took out the bowels,
But deftly, not to destroy the first knot.
They gripped the gullet hard, swiftly severed
The weasand from the wind-pipe, and shucked out the guts.
They sheared off the shoulders with their sharp knives
And poked the bones through slits, preserving the sides.
They rent the breast, pulled the bones wide apart,
Then got to work on the gullet. One   1340
Ripped it swiftly, right up to the leg-forks,
Nimbly cleaned out the innards; then they commenced
To free all the fillets that ran along the ribs.
They cleaned the back-bones quite correctly
In a straight sweep, down to the hanging haunch,
Lifted the haunch up whole, and lopped it off.
The loose parts, properly speaking, men call the *mumbles*.

      Right down
    The leg-forks they released
    The flesh on every one,   1350
    And quickly split each beast
    Along the long back-bone.

And then they hewed off both the head and neck,
And, with a chop, severed the sides from the chine.
They kept a tidbit for the crows, tossed it into the trees,
Then rent a hole in the full flanks near the ribs
And hung the beast from branches by the hocks.
Each huntsman was handed his proper portion
While their dogs feasted hungrily on a fine doe-skin,
On the lights and liver, the lining of the paunches,   1360
And on bread sopped in the blood that spilled around.
The kill was boldly blown, the hounds bayed loudly,

[49]

And all headed for home, their meat packed up neatly,
Proudly sounding all their hunting horns.
By then the day was done, and the company came
Into the lovely hall where the knight was quietly waiting,
    beside
    A dancing fire at the hearth.
    The lord enters with pride,
    And when they meet there's mirth   1370
    And joy on every side.

The lord commanded all the men to come to the hall
And bade both the ladies down, with their maids-in-waiting.
Before all the folk in the hall he orders his hunters
To fetch his venison and set it before him on the floor.
With gracious ceremony he summons Gawain
And tells the tale of all the animals he's slain;
He shows him the fine flesh hewn from the ribs:
'What do you say to that for sport? Is it worth your praise?
Do I deserve your thanks for my skill at the hunt?'   1380
'Before God,' said Gawain, 'these are the finest beasts
I've seen for seven years in a winter season.'
'I give them all to you, Gawain,' was the lord's answer,
'Our contract agrees you can claim them as your own.'
'That's right,' he replied, 'and I say the same to you.
What I have won with all honour, here in your hall,
Is yours indeed, as we agreed. I give it with goodwill.'
Now he clasps him with both arms around the neck
And kisses him as courteously as he can.
'There, take my trophies for I got no more than that,   1390
Had they been greater I'd gladly give them to you.'
'That's very fine,' replied the lord, 'Many thanks, but maybe

They were greater—so I wish you would tell me where,
With your subtlety, you won such a wonderful prize.'
'That's not part of the pact,' he said, 'ask me no more.
You've received what's yours. That's all, you may rest
   assured.'
  They laughed, and ribbed each other
  With many a jaunty word,
  Then went to dine together   1400
  Where fine food steamed on the board.

After that they both sat together before the fire
Where the women brought them beakers of wine;
And, in their raillery, they decided to repeat
Next day the same bargain they had made before:
Whatever happened, they would hand their winnings over,
Exchanging at night the new things they had gained.
Both of them gave their oath before the gathering.
More beverages were brought, and their mirth re-kindled.
Then, at last, the lords and the ladies left,   1410
Bidding goodnight, and quickly repaired to their bedrooms.
The rooster had not roused, cackled and crowed three times*
Before the lord leapt from his bed, and his men too.
Once more, both Mass and meal were quickly over
And, before daybreak, off to the forest in their hunting array
   they hurry.
  Sounds of their hunting-horns
  Over the wide plains carry
  To the hounds, loosed among thorns,
  Who hurtle towards their quarry.   1420

Soon they mount a search at the edge of a marsh,
The huntsmen goading the hounds that had the scent,

Rousing them fiercely, raising a frightful din.
The hounds, hearing the shouts, hurried forward
And sprang along the trail, a throng of forty or so,
And such a riot of yelps and yaps arose
That all the rocks around rang with the sound.
The hunters, with shouts and horn-blasts, urged them on.
At that, the pack strung together and sprinted
Down a track between a pool and a beetling crag.   1430
By the edge of a rock outcrop, near the marsh's rim,
Where rough rocks had fallen hugger-mugger,
They rushed in to flush their quarry, the hunters following.
They spread around the crag and the jagged mound
Till they were certain they'd trapped inside their circle
The beast that the bloodhounds had discovered.
Then they beat the bushes furiously, forcing him out.
Maddened, he charged at the men that checked his way,
Barrelling out, the most marvellous boar:*
A long-time loner, cut off from his kind,*   1440
But still a redoubtable beast, the stoutest of boars,
Grunting at them grimly, and they were all dismayed
For, with his first thrust, he destroyed three dogs*
Then, in no way hurt himself, spurted away.
The men shouted 'Ho!' very loudly, again and again;
Set horns to their mouths, sounded the hunting-call,
And joyful cries rose from the milling hounds
And men, as they ran at the boar in a swelling roar
          of sound.
          He stops often, and growls,   1450
          Then jabs at the pack around;
          There are horrible yelps and yowls
          Each time he maims a hound.

Then the men push forward to fire arrows at him;
They loosed the long shafts, struck him in showers,
But the tips were knocked aside by his tough hide
And no point could pierce his bristling brow;
Though the smooth-shaven shafts were shattered to pieces,
As soon as they hit him, the heads slewed off.
Then, under the welter of their pelting arrow-blows,   1460
Crazed by their baiting, he hurled himself at the hunters,
Goring them savagely as he bored forward.
Many among them were fearful, and they fell back.
But the lord, on a light horse, gallops at him hard;
Like a bold knight on a battlefield, he blows his bugle,
Sounding the rally as he rides through bush and briar
Chasing the doughty boar till, once more, darkness came.
In this way they pass the whole day at the hunt,
While our gracious knight reclines at his leisure,
In luxurious pleasure, under bed-covers rich and   1470
          bright-hued.
     Nor was the lady neglecting
     To greet him in this mood,
     For she came again—expecting
     To change his attitude.

She creeps to the curtain, peeps in at the knight.
Gawain gave her first a cordial greeting,
And she, polite and eager, replied in kind.
She sat down lightly beside him, laughing;
Then, with a loving look, she started speaking: 1480
'If you are Gawain, sir, it seems to me most strange
That, being inclined to breeding and fine manners,
You've no patience with the ways of polite society,

[53]

Or, being taught them, banish them from your thoughts.
For you have surely forgotten what I showed you yesterday
In the finest lesson that my lips could form.'
'And what was that?' said the man, 'for I am unaware
Of it. But if it be true, I am much to blame.'
'But I taught you to kiss,' the kind lady said,
'To make your claim quickly when the lady is willing;   1490
Such behaviour becomes every knight who earns the name.'
'Dear lady, don't say such things,' the man said.
'I dare not do that for fear of being refused—
For, if refused, my offer would wear a fool's face.'
'In honesty, none could refuse you,' she nobly replied,
'And, of couse, you have the sinew to subdue by force
Those churlish enough to wish to rebuff you.'
Gawain agreed. 'Indeed, what you say is true
But such force is unworthy in one of Arthur's court,
As is a gift not made with goodwill in mind.   1500
But see, I'm at your command, to kiss as you please:
You may take one when you like and leave off at
                your whim.'
        She graciously leans his way
        And neatly kisses him—
        And of love's turnings they say
        Much in the interim.

'Now, if you won't be angry with me,' she went on,
'I would like to learn from you, sir. How does it happen
That one so young and lively as you, so active,   1510
So courteous and chivalrous, so esteemed in every house,
And of all chivalrous deeds, if one need choose, the chief—
Don't you agree?—are the deeds of love and war,

[54]

For the text and the very title of those volumes*
Which deal with knightly deeds describe in detail how
Have hazarded their lives in the cause of love,
Suffered for love's sake long ordeals, then
Avenged themselves with valour, vanquished sorrow
And brought great joy to a lady's bedroom,
And you, known as the noblest knight in all the land,   1520
Your fame and honour following you everywhere—
How does it happen that I have sat beside you twice
Right here, and never heard the smallest word from you
About love-lore—not the least little thing.
Now, one so courteous and correct in his vows,
Would, I think, be yearning to show a young woman
At least a tiny token of the crafts of love.
Does it mean, despite your fame, you're in the dark?
Or do you think—shame on you!—I'm too slow to follow?
      Not so!   1530
    I've come alone to sit
    And learn new ways. Please show
    The treasures of your wit.
    My lord, being gone, won't know.'

'In good faith,' murmured Gawain, 'may God reward you!
It gives one great pleasure—great gladness—
That one so worthy as you should come to this room
And take pains with so poor a person, and sport
With your knight—I'm flattered by your fine favours.
But to take on the task of explaining true love,   1540
To discourse, moreover, on the themes of love and war
To you, who, without doubt, are as deft
In that fine art as an army of fellows like me

[55]

Will ever be, even if we live long lives—
That would be stupid, esteemed lady, in the extreme.
I'll grant your other requests to the best of my skill
For I am deeply beholden, and will always be
Your loyal servant, may the Lord save me.'
This way, whatever other motive she had in mind,
The lady lured him on, enticing him to sin.   1550
But he held himself back so well no blemish appeared.
There was no sin on either side, nothing but innocent
      pleasure.
      They laughed. She lingered on;
      And then, taking her measure,
      Kissed him—and thereupon
      Gracefully left, at her leisure.

Now the knight gets up and goes to Mass;
The morning meal was cooked and served with ceremony.
Then, all day long, Gawain amused himself with the ladies   1560
While the lord galloped and cantered over his lands,
Chasing the wild boar that raced over the banks
And bit the best of his hounds, cracking their backs.
When he stood at bay the bowmen broke his will;
Gathering in groups, they shot shock-volleys of arrows,
Forced him to flee, to go for the open ground.
He could still make the hardiest start aside.
But in the end he was spent and could spurt no more
So, quick as he could, he gained higher ground
And found a hole near a rock, where the river ran by.   1570
He got the bank at his back, began to scrape,
A foul cud foaming at the corners of his mouth
As he honed his tusks. The hunters hovered, held back,

Weary of wounding him from afar, but still afraid.
He'd hurt so many hunters. Close in now? No one would
       that task.
    No sense at all in waging
    More lives on such a risk
    With his mad brain raging
    Behind that murderous tusk.   1580

Then the lord surged up, spurring his steed fiercely,
And saw him standing at bay, surrounded by hunters.
He leaps down lightly, leaves his mount,
Unsheathes a bright sword,* strides forward,
Quickly wades the stream to where the beast waits
Watching the man warily as he lifts the weapon.
His big bristles stood up, and he snorted so loud
They were much afraid the lord might be worsted.
Then the boar made a rush, right at the man,
And with a crash they tumbled together, splashing   1590
In white water. But the beast was defeated.
Right from the start the man had sighted him well
And he drove the big blade deep into his chest,
Shoved it in to the hilt, shattering the heart.
He crashed over. The water washed him away, with his
       last growls.
    Quickly, before he sank,
    In a splash of yelps and howls,
    He was dragged onto the bank
    And rent by a hundred jowls.   1600

They blew the death of the boar with a blare of horns;
Every man shouted and hallooed, loud as he could.

[57]

The huntsmen placed in charge of that hard chase
Had their hounds bay at the beast.
Then one of them, wise in the crafts of the wood,
Began with elegant care to cut up the boar.
First he hacks off the head, sets it up high,
Then splits him roughly right along the spine,
Uncoils the bowels, roasts them on red-hot coals,
Dunks bread-sops in them, divides them among his dogs;   1610
Then slices the boar-flesh into broad gleaming slabs,
Pulls out the guts, and cuts them away, as is proper.
Then sews the two halves in a single whole.
Then they truss him up on a stout stick.
Now, with their swine hanging, they swing off homeward.
The boar's head* was borne before the lord himself,
Who had dealt the death-blow in the stream after that swift
        mêlée.
    It seemed to him, till he saw
    Gawain, a long delay.   1620
    Then he called him and once more
    The knight came for his pay.

The lord laughed loudly and merrily then;
He greeted sir Gawain, and joked with him joyfully.
The good ladies were called, the whole house gathered.
He points to the pieces of boar-flesh, tells them the tale
Of his great mass and vast length, how malicious he was,
And how wildly he'd fought as he fled into the woods.
Gawain hastened to praise his hunting prowess;
He commended the skills he'd so clearly displayed,   1630
For a beast of such bulk and muscle, he maintained,
Or with such broad flanks, he'd not seen before.

[58]

They patted the huge head, praised it again,
Recoiled, feigning fear, so that the lord might hear.
'Now, Gawain,' said the good man, 'as you know, this game,
By our fixed and final contract, is yours completely.'
'True,' he replied, 'and by our terms it's also right
That I must give you back the gains that are mine.'
He clasped the knight round the neck, and kissed him.
Then straightway served him again in the same way.   1640
'This evening,' said Gawain, 'we're still even, you see,
In all the covenants that, since my coming, we
       have made.'
    'By Saint Giles!'* the lord said,
    'What a fine game you've played!
    You'll heap wealth on your head
    If you conduct such trade.'

The serving-men then set up trestle-tables,
And spread white cloths over them. Clear light
Gleamed on walls as the servants set waxen torches,   1650
And then brought food for all the folk in the hall.
A happy murmuring arose, then merry music
And mirth around the hearth. All sorts of singing
During the dinner, and after, rang through the room:
Old Christmas tunes and the newest carols and dances,
The most delightful pleasures a man could describe.
And our handsome knight stayed close beside the lady
Who dallied with him, offering subtle sallies,
Giving furtive and fetching glances, and he
Was caught in confusion, vexed in himself, perplexed;   1660
But, out of good breeding, he decided not to rebuff her,
But to deal with her delicately, though his plan might go

[59]

awry;
    They stayed on in that way
    Till the end of their revelry,
    Then the lord called him away
    For some fire-side causerie.

And there they drank and debated, deciding anew
The self-same terms for tomorrow, New Year's Eve;
The knight begged permission to depart next morning   1670
As it was now approaching the hour when he must go;
But to little avail, for the lord prevailed upon him:
'Stay,' he replied, 'I assure you, hand on heart,
You'll get to the Green Chapel and achieve your errand
On time, on the morn of New Year's Day, well before prime,
So rest in peace in your room, be at your ease
While I hunt in the holt and keep the covenant
To exchange my gains with you when I get home.
I have tested you twice and I have found you true
But "*third time, winner takes all*"—recall my words   1680
Tomorrow. Meanwhile, let's have more merriment,
For a man can find misery whenever he wants.'
Gawain agreed to that, and agreed to remain there.
Drinks were brought, then torches when the day
            was done.
    As if rocked on a raft,
    Gawain sleeps on and on.
    The lord, intent on his craft,
    Rises at earliest dawn.

After Mass, he and his men took a quick mouthful.   1690
A magnificent morning! He calls for his mount.

All the hunters who would follow him on horse
Were girt up and in saddle at the castle gates.
Fresh light over the fields: frost on the ground,
Sun climbing through a wrack of ruddy clouds,
Dissolving them in wide light, driving them off.
The huntsmen loosed their hounds by a leafy wood
And the rocks rang with the sound of hunting horns.
Some sniffed the trail down which the fox lay lurking,*
And cunningly crossed it, weaving about, in their way.   1700
A small whelp smells him, and yelps; the hunters call.
Up come his companions, panting madly
And, packed together, they take off on his tracks.
The fox flicks ahead of them; they soon sight him
And they're after him again fast as they can go,
Deriding him fiercely, with a furious din.
He twists quickly through a tangled thicket,
Then edges back, and bides his time in a hedge;
He hops over a hawthorn thicket by a small stream
And slinks out stealthily through the valley,   1710
Hoping to outwit the hounds and escape in the woods;
Suddenly, before him stood a band of hunters
By a gap in the trees, and three growling hounds,
     all grey.
    He twisted back, with a start,
    And boldly sprang away
    To the woods, fear at his heart,
    The smell of death in the day.

When the pack gathered, and put him up,
What a din! A delicious pleasure to hear those dogs!   1720
When he veered into view they abused him bitterly,

A sound as if the cliffs were crashing down.
And the huntsmen hallooed mightily when they met him.
He was greeted with snarling snouts, and growls;
He was threatened, called 'cur' and 'thief';
And the dogs closed on his tail so he couldn't delay.
When he sped, going for open ground, he was headed off;
So he wound back, rapidly—Reynard* was so wily.
In this way, he led them all astray, the lord and
His men, till the height of morning, among the mountains.   1730
In his room at home the knight sleeps soundly
In the cold morning, ringed by rich awnings.
But, for love's sake, the lady was awake,
Nursing her heart's wish, lest her will weaken.
She suddenly got up, and went on her way
In a bright gown that brushed the ground lightly;
It was hemmed and lined with the finest fur.
She wore no head-piece, but in her hair-net were
Studded gem-stones, in clusters of twenty or so.
Her fair face and her throat were both   1740
Quite bare, and her breast and her white shoulders.
She deftly enters the bedroom. The door behind her
Closes; she throws wide the window,* calls the knight
To rouse him with her rich voice and joyful words:
> 'I say,
> How can you sleep, good sir,
> On such a splendid day?'
> He heard, through a drowsy blur,
> Her words wafting his way.

Drugged with heavy dreams, the man muttered   1750
As one who, on waking, is shaken by the thought

That today his fate would gaze into his face
At the Green Chapel, where he must meet that man
And withstand his foul axe, and not fight back.
But soon as he had summoned his reason
He broke from his reverie and replied to her brightly.
The lady approaches the bed, laughs pertly,
Leans over, and lightly kisses his lips,
And he greets her warmly, in a most grateful manner.
He saw she looked lovely in her rich robes,   1760
Her features flawless, and her colour so fine
It warmed his blood, and a great blessedness welled up
In him. They smiled shyly, prattled on merrily,
And all was bliss between them, all joy
      and light.
    Their speech was calm and clear
    And everything stood right.
    Yet danger was waiting near
    Should Mary neglect her knight.

For that lovely lady pressed him hard, persisted   1770
Urgently, spurring him to the brink, and he thinks:
'I must accept her affection, or refuse, and offend her',
Concerned with courtesy, lest he be thought a boor,
But more concerned about a misdeed should he err
And betray the man to whom the hall belonged.
'God help me,' he thought, 'that's not going to happen!'
With a short laugh he lightly laid aside
All the fine phrases that tripped from her tongue.
'You merit much blame,' exclaimed the lady,
'If you lack love for the person you lie beside   1780
Who is hurt now beyond anyone in the world.

[63]

Perhaps you already love a lady and, preferring her,
You've pledged your word, promised her so firmly
You cannot break it—that's what I've come to believe.
Is it true? Be honest with me, I beg of you.
Don't disguise truth with guile, for all the love
        on earth.'
      'I have no love, by St John,*
      I swear for all I'm worth!
      No one at all—and need no one   1790
      Right now,' he replied in mirth.

'That's the worst word of all,' the woman said.
'But you have given a true answer, and it grieves me.
Come, kiss me quickly, then I must hasten away.
I must go on in sorrow, as a woman will who has loved.'
Sighing, she leans across and lightly kisses him;
Then goes her way, saying as she gets up,
'Now, my dear, as I depart allow me this:
Please give me a small present—a glove perhaps—
To remember you by, and rid myself of my grief.'   1800
'By Heaven,' he said, 'I wish I had something worthy
Of your loving friendship—the finest gift in the land!
Truth to tell, you deserve much more,
By rights, than any gift that I might give.
But a love-token would be of little avail,
A dubious honour indeed, to hold in your house—
A glove of Gawain as a keepsake in your care!
I have come here on a quest through rough country
And have no bearers with saddle-bags full of fine things.
Because of your love, that distresses me, dear lady.   1810
But each man as he can. Please, it's no impoliteness that

I offer.'
'No, no—but since, sweet knight,
You've no gift for my coffer,'
Said the lady, 'it is right
You take whatever I proffer.'

She gave him a ring wrought in red gold.
On it, a glittering stone stood out
That gleamed with light-beams, bright as the sun.
Be assured it was worth a fine fortune.*   1820
Nevertheless, the knight refused it, replying nimbly:
'I cannot take gifts at this time, good lady,
For I really may not tend you anything in return.'
She importuned him eagerly; again he refused
And swore, as before, he could and would not accept it.
Regretting his refusal, she then replied:
'If you refuse my ring because it appears costly
And because you'll feel yourself deeply beholden,
I shall give you my girdle, a gift of lesser worth.'
She loosed a belt she wore about her waist   1830
Looped round her gown under her lovely mantle.
It was of green silk, sewn with a trim of gold,
Its margins highly embroidered by a fine hand.
She pleaded with him once more, with pleasant smiles,
That he might take it, unworthy as it was for a knight.
And he told her he would never even touch
Keepsake or gold, till God had sent him grace
Or before he had finished the task he had taken on.
'And now, I pray you, do not be displeased,
And do stop pressing me. My mind is firm. To that, pray be   1840
                resigned.

[65]

Yet I am deeply beholden
For you have been so kind;
Through times dark or golden
I'll serve you with heart and mind.'

'Do you refuse my girdle,' the lady replied,
'Because it is so simple? It may well seem so.
A poor rag, really—a most improper gift.
Yet the person who knows the power of its knots
Would perhaps gauge it at a greater price,   1850
For with this green lace girt about his waist,
While he keeps it closely wound around him
He cannot be cut down by any man nor slain
By any cleverness or cunning under the whole Heavens.'
The knight, pondering her words, now began to wonder
If it might be a talisman in his terrible plight
When he came to the Green Chapel to get his gains:
Maybe death could be foiled with this marvellous device!
Patient now as she pressed him, he allowed her to speak.
She gave him the girdle once more, most eagerly.   1860
He accepted, and she granted the gift with goodwill
And besought him, for her sake, never to uncover it
But loyally to conceal it from her lord. He conceded:*
No one will know except themselves, no matter what
          the price.
          He thanked her, time and again,
          For her gift and her advice.
          By then she had kissed Gawain
          The hardy, not once, but thrice.

The lady makes ready to go and leave him be   1870

[66]

For she knows she'll get no greater satisfaction.
When she has gone Gawain gets up from the bed
And dresses in the best and richest raiment.
He hides the love-lace that the lady gave him,
Conceals it carefully where he can find it later,
Then rapidly makes his way towards the chapel,
Goes to a priest in private and beseeches him
To instruct him how to conduct his life and learn
How his soul might be saved when he leaves the earth.
Then he fully confessed, admitting his misdeeds,   1880
Both large and lesser, and begged for mercy,
And he also called on the priest for absolution.
He absolved him completely, so wholly cleansed him
That it might have been the dawning of Judgement Day.*
Then he was free to please himself and the ladies
At carols and dancing and delightful pleasures
Much more than ever before, till the fall
        of night.
        Each man he honoured there
        And all exclaimed outright: 1890
        'I think, since his coming here,
        He has never shone so bright.'

LET him stay in that haven, may love come his way!
The lord is still at his sport in the far fields.
He has finished off the fox he'd followed so long:*
As he leapt over the hedgerow to look at the rascal
At a place where the hounds were giving hot chase,
Reynard ran quickly through a thicket
With the yapping rabble hard at his heels.
The lord, catching sight of the wild creature, slyly   1900

[67]

Waited, withdrew a bright sword, and struck.
He shied away from the sharp blade, tried to evade him,
But the hounds rushed at him before he could run back
And fell on him in front of the horse's feet
And harried their clever quarry, snapping and snarling.
The lord leaps down and lifts him by the pelt,
Snatches him out briskly from their busy snouts,
Holds him above his head, and bellows 'Halloo',
And the fretting hounds mill round, barking furiously.
The hunters, with their many horns, hurry along   1910
Rightly sounding the rally, till they recognize their lord.
By then the noble men of the company were coming up
And those who carried bugles blew them and cried out
And those who had no horns bellowed and hallooed:
The most cheering cry that a man might hear.
They roared for the soul of Reynard—a resounding
        full note.
        The dogs are fondly praised
        With strokes on head and throat,
        And then Reynard is raised   1920
        And stripped of his tawny coat.*

Then, with nightfall nearing, they headed home,
Proudly blowing on their stout bugles.
At last the lord dismounts by his beloved castle,
Where he finds a fire in the hearth, the knight beside it,
The good man, sir Gawain, whose heart was glad
As he'd treasured the love of the ladies in full measure.
His robe of rich blue reached to the ground,
And he looked fine in a surcoat, softly furred.
A mantling hood, that matched it, hung from his shoulders,   1930

[68]

Both trimmed with fur from the finest ermine.
He rose, met his host in the middle of the room,
Greeted him with great pleasure, exclaiming:
'This time, my lord, I'm first to keep our agreement
Which we made final that time when the wine was flowing.'
Then he embraces the knight and kisses him thrice
With as much energy and glee as he could muster.
'By Heaven,' said the lord, 'you've had enormous luck
In gaining that booty, if you drove a good bargain.'
'Don't bother your head about bargains,' he said.   1940
'I've openly returned whatever, by rights, I owe you.'
'By Mary, mine are much less impressive,'
Said the lord. 'I worked a long day and won nothing.
A miserable fox-fur, may the Devil take it!
A paltry reward to pay for such riches!
And you have given me three kisses that no man can
            excel.'
        'By the Cross, our bargain's good,'
        Said Gawain. 'I thank you well.'
        The lord, right where they stood,   1950
        Told how the bold fox fell.

With mirth, music and the finest fare,
They made as merry as any man might
And they laughed with the ladies, joked and jested.
Gawain and his host were most happy indeed
Like men who are light-headed, or a little tipsy.
The lord and his retinue played plenty of ruses
Till the time fell for the last farewell
And for all to go from the hall and be off to bed.
Gawain turns, and graciously takes his leave of the lord,   1960

[69]

Greeting that noble knight with gratitude:
'May I give you thanks for this marvellous time,
And God bless you for your great honours at this feast.
Were you willing, I'd yield myself up as your man,
But, as you know, I must go on in the morning.
Please grant me, as you promised, a guide to lead me
To the gate of the Green Chapel, where God
Would have me face my fate on New Year's Day.'
'Indeed,' he said, 'I did agree to that, and you'll see
My promise fulfilled perfectly, and with pleasure.'   1970
He promptly singles out a servant to point the way
And direct him over the dales with the least delay
By a quick path that goes through thickets and groves
                    of trees.
          The lord, for his uncommon
          And countless courtesies,
          He thanked, and the noble women,
          And gave them his good-byes.

He spoke to them softly, his heart heavy,
And kissed them, expressing great gratitude for their   1980
    kindness,
And they, in turn, gave him their compliments,
Commending him to Christ, with grave sighs.
Now he courteously takes his leave of that noble company;
He spoke a warming word to each man he stood before
For his fine service, and the trouble he had taken,
And for tending him so faithfully all that time.
And each man there was as sorry to see him go
As if they had lived their whole lives with him.
Servants, bearing lights, led him to his bedroom

And, as he needed sleep, brought him to bed.   1990
Whether, once there, he slept, I dare not say,
For the morning was much on his mind as he thought
            and thought.
    Let him lie there and wait,
    He almost has what he sought.
    If you're patient, I'll relate
    All that the morning brought.

IV

Night passes and New Year's Day draws near,
Dawn drives out the dark as the Lord decrees.
A time of wild weather; the wind increases,   2000
Clouds rain down over the cold ground;
A nagging northerly pinches the skin,   *annoying*
Blown snow whips about, nipping the animals;
Wind whistles in gusts and howls off the heights,
Packing the dales with deep drifting snow.
Lying wide awake, the knight listens:
At each cock-crow he told the time exactly.
Though he closed his eyelids he dozed but little.
Before first light he leapt briskly out of bed,
For a lamp still burned on in the bedroom.   2010
He roused his chamberlain, who replied straightway.
He bade him bring his suit of mail, and his saddle.
The man gets up, goes to fetch his clothes for him,
Then soon arrays sir Gawain in splendid style,
Beginning with warm clothes against the biting cold,
Then his mail-armour, which the men had safely stored:
Chest-pieces, plate-armour perfectly polished,
And his coat of mail, its metal rings rubbed clean of rust.*
All seemed brand new and he was thankful
   indeed.   2020
  As he buckled on each piece
  It shone like a burnished bead,
  The finest from here to Greece.
  Then he asked for his steed.

Gawain arranged the best of the gear himself:
His coat-armour, its crest a bright blazon
Worked in velvet, with vivid gems pointing the virtues,
Beaten and beautifully set, with embroidered seams
And a marvellous lining of finest fur.
Nor did he leave off the lace-girdle, the lady's gift;   2030
For his own good, Gawain could not forget that.
When he'd buckled his blade about his firm haunches
He wound his love-token twice around him,*
Tucked it quickly about his waist, content
That the green silk-girdle suited him well;
Against its ground of royal red it glowed richly.
But he wore the green belt not for its beauty
Nor for its pendants, all neatly polished,
Nor for the gold that glinted on its end-knots,
But to save himself when it behoved him to suffer   2040
And stand defenceless against death when he met that man
        again.
    Now that he is ready
    He strides outside, and then
    He turns and, in a body,
    Thanks all the serving-men.

His great horse Gringolet was waiting for him.
He had been proudly stabled; he stood there, towering,
Fretting at the reins, fit—and itching to be off.
The knight strode up to him, studied his coat   2050
And muttered softly, swearing on his oath,
'Here are men who care, and mind about honour.
Much happiness to the man who maintains these men.
And may the fine lady find happiness and long life.

Whenever they cherish a guest out of their charity
Heaping honour on their heads, may the Lord
In High Heaven reward them, and all in this hall!
If I am still to dwell on this earth a while
I will certainly, God willing, return with a great gift.'
He steps up into the stirrup, bestrides the big horse.   2060
His man hands him his shield; he slings it over his shoulder.
With the spikes of his gilt heels he spurs Gringolet
Who springs off at once—no more need to prance on the stones
          and rear.
          Now man and horse ride tall
          And the man bears lance and spear.
          'May Christ protect this hall;
          May all things prosper here.'

The bridge was drawn down, the wide gates
Unbarred. Both halves slowly opened.   2070
As he crossed the bridge-boards the knight blessed himself.
He praised the porter, who knelt before the knight
To give him good day and pray God to keep him;
Then went off on his way with his one attendant
To point out the route to that perilous place
Where soon he must suffer that mighty blow.
They rode by bank-sides under bare branches,
They climbed by cliffs where the cold hung.
Clouds, high overhead; down below, danger.
Mist drizzled on the moors, dissolved the summits.   2080
Each peak wore a hat, a huge mist-mantle.
Brook-waters boiled, sluiced over the slopes;
White water raged against the river-banks.
The way they took through the woods was wild,

[74]

But soon it was time for the morning sun to
      come up.
   In a field of fresh snow
   That lay on a high hill-top
   The servant reined in, and now
   Bade his master stop.   2090

'See, I have come this distance with you, sir,
And you are not far now from the notable place
That you have sought so long and so zealously.
But I shall tell you the truth as I know you well
And as you are a much-loved lord and man;
If you observe my words to the letter you'll be better served.
The place you're headed for is held to be perilous
For in those wastes lives the worst man in the world.
He is fearless and brutal and delights in fighting;
He is mightier than any man you might imagine.   2100
His body is bulkier than four of the best
In Arthur's house, or Hector's,* or any man's.
He chooses to challenge whoever might appear
At the Green Chapel; however skilled at arms
He will put him down, destroy him with one blow.
For he is vicious; his violence knows no mercy:
Whether churl or chaplain rides by his church,
Whether monk, or priest, or any other man,*
He thrives on killing them all, as he loves his life.
So I tell you as truly as you sit upon that saddle   2110
Go if you will—but, if he has his way, you'll be slain.
Believe me, though you have twenty lives to trade for
     your own:
   He's lived here since long ago;

[75]

In fights he cuts all down;
Against his deadly blow
No sure defence is known.

So it's wise, sir Gawain, to leave him be.
When you go, for God's sake take a different track.
Ride home through another region, where Christ can help
    you.   2120
I'll hurry home meanwhile, and I promise
And swear, by God and all his good saints—
So help me!—and by the holy relics and all else,
To keep your secret loyally, and tell no one you ran
From any knight or man that's known to me.'
'Many thanks,' he murmured, then replied somewhat drily,
'I'm touched by your care for my welfare. I wish you well.
I'm sure you'd keep my secret quite securely,
But however firmly you held it, should I fail here
And scuttle off, fleeing in fright, as you suggest,   2130
I'd be a fraud and coward, and could not be forgiven.
No—I shall go to the chapel, whatever happens,
And say to the man you speak of whatever I wish,
Come foul fortune or good, wherever my fate
           might dwell.
      Tough he may be, his arm
      Might wield a club that can kill,
      But the Lord will save from harm
      All those who serve Him well.'

'Mother of God!' cried the man, 'if your mind's made up   2140
To take your troubles entirely on your head—
If you wish to lose your life, I won't argue.

[76]

Put on your helmet, hold your spear at your side
And ride down the track that takes you close to that cliff;
Descend to the very depths of that wild valley
Then glance a little around the glade; on your left hand,
Chance is, you will see that self-same chapel
And its massive master, grimly guarding it.
Farewell, noble Gawain, for I would not
Keep you company for all the gold in the ground   2150
Nor walk with you one foot further through this wood.'   *death*
Brusquely, the man wrenches his bridle around,   *danger in*
Kicks his horse with his heels, quick and hard,   *wood*
And gallops off and away, leaving Gawain
          still there.*
      'I'll neither groan nor weep,'
      Muttered the knight, 'I swear.
      It's God's will: I must keep
      My word, and not despair.'

He goads Gringolet further on, follows the path,   2160
Rides along a bank beside a forest-fringe,
Negotiates a steep slope down into a dale.
He surveys the scene; it seems to him dreary, wild—
No place to hide, no haven to protect him,
But on both sides, sheer beetling banks:
Rough crags and piles of jagged rocks
Like snapped spears that appeared to scratch the sky.
He halted, reined in his horse, rested a moment,
Gazing around for a glimpse of the Green Chapel.
He thought it strange that nothing caught his notice,   2170
Save something a short way off, where a kind of mound
Rose up, a barrow* on a slope by a flowing stream

Where a rushing waterfall ran down. There,
The stream bubbled; it seemed to be boiling.
The man forced his horse towards the mound,
And leapt off lightly by a linden tree.
He hitched his horse's bridle to a rough branch,
Stalked over to the mound and walked around it,
Wondering what on earth such a barrow could be.
Both at the end and sides it had big vents,   2180
The bump completely grown over with clumps of grass;
And nothing inside, save the deep dark of a cave,
Or the crevice of an old crag—he couldn't tell which
                    from there.
          'The Green Chapel! Lord, what a sight!
          A place, more likely, where
          In the dark of midnight
          The Devil says morning prayer.

'An utter desert,' muttered Gawain. 'What a desolation,
With its sinister shrine, and tufts of weed everywhere!   2190
A fitting spot for that fellow in his green gown
To do his devil's rites and unholy duties!
All my five senses say it is the Fiend
Who's brought me down here to destroy me!*
What an unhappy place! An evil chapel—Devil
Take this accursed church, the worst I've ever chanced on.'
His helmet firm on his head, lance in hand,
He strode up to the roof of that rough abode.
At that height, from behind a boulder, he heard
Way off, beyond the brook, a weird sound.   2200
Listen to that! It clattered against cliffs, as if to shatter them:
A sound like a scythe being ground against a stone.

[78]

Listen! It sang, and whirred, like wild mill-water
In a race.* It clanged and rang out, rushing
Towards him. 'By God, this instrument is meant
To honour me alone; it is for me he hones
      his blade!
    God's will be done. To cry
    "Alas" is of little aid.
    Yet, even if I'm to die,   *do not fear death*   2210
    No noise will make me afraid.'

With that, the knight called out with all his might:
'Who's master here, who keeps his covenant with me?'
Without halting, Gawain stalks up to the place:
'If anyone wants anything let him walk out now,
And finish this business off—now or never.'
'Be patient,' came a call from the bank above him.
'You'll very soon get what I promised you.'
The sound went on again as he ground for a while.
The grind-stone whined, then stopped; and the man   2220
Stepped down, wound his way by a crag, and whirled
Out of a gap in the rock-wall with a grisly weapon:
Danish-made, its bright blade whetted for the blow,
Colossal and sharp, its shaft cunningly shaped.
Gauged by the gleaming lace he gripped it by
It was all of four feet broad, or more.
And the man in green was dressed as he'd seen him first:
The same bushy beard, thick thighs, and hair
Hanging down—save now he saunters firmly on foot
Wielding his weapon like a walking stick.   2230
When he reached the water he refused to wade across
But vaulted over on the huge handle, not halting,

But striding, fiercely angry, over a wide field
        of snow.
    And Gawain bowed his head,
    In greeting—but not too low.
    'Well, sir,' the other said,
    'I see you can keep your vow.'

'Gawain,' said the green knight, 'may God protect you.
I wish you a pleasant welcome to my place!   2240
You've judged your journey well, as a true man should,
And you're perfectly correct on the pact we agreed upon:
A twelvemonth ago, you took what fell to you then;
Now, on this New Year's Day I shall pay you back.
We're on our own down here in this lonely dale,
No man stands between us, we can strike as bitterly as
We please. Take your helm from your head. Prepare yourself!
And do not resist for I didn't restrain you
When you hacked my head off with your first smack.'
'By the God who gave me soul and spirit,   2250
I shan't begrudge you your blow nor any harm that happens.
But take one stroke only; I'll stand still meanwhile.
Do whatever you wish—I'll neither resist
        nor care.'
    He dropped his head, waiting.
    His neck showed white and bare,
    He made as if this thing
    Would never cause him fear.

Now the man in green gets ready, steadies himself,
Sweeps back the grim weapon to hack at Gawain.   2260
He flourishes it with all the force in his big body

And brings down a dreadful blow, as if to destroy him.
Had it descended as hard as he seemed to intend
He would have been bisected by that blow,
But Gawain, glancing sideways as the axe swung,
Flinched his shoulders to evade the sharp blade
As it flashed towards the flint to topple him.
Suddenly the man in green stopped his motion
Then scolded him with a spate of fine phrases:
'You're not Gawain,' he said, 'so noble and so good.*   2270
He's not afraid of a whole army by hill or dale.
And now you tremble in terror even before I touch you.
I never knew he was such a lily-livered knight!
Did I flinch, or flee from you when your blow felled me?
Did I cavil, or create a fuss at King Arthur's house?
My head flew to my feet but I never flicked an eyebrow;
And you—I haven't even touched you and you're trembling.
It's clear I'm the better man here, the case is white
          and black.'
          Gawain replied: 'Enough!   2280
          I won't flinch when you hack—
          Though once my head is off
          I cannot put it back.

'But swing promptly, man, and bring me to your point.
Deliver me to my destiny—but don't delay!
I'll stand up to your stroke and start away no more
Till your steel strike me squarely. There's my oath on it.'
'Here is your bargain, then!' He heaved the blade up high
And gazed at him savagely as if somewhat crazed.
He gathered himself for a great blow, then held   2290
His hand, letting him stand there, still unharmed.

[81]

Gawain readied himself, steady in every limb,
Still as a stone, or the stump of a tree
That grips the rocky ground with a hundred roots.
The man in green chatted on cheerily, mocking him:
'Now you've recovered your nerve I have to hit you.
May the great knighthood of King Arthur guard you
And keep your neck-bone from this blow—if it can.'
Gawain, afire with fierce rage, replied,
'Get on, man. No more threatening. Strike!   2300
It seems to me you've made yourself afraid.'
'All right,' the knight said, 'after such a speech
I'll no longer delay your quest, nor let you break
        your vow.'
        He stands ready to swing,
        Face puckered. Imagine how
        Gawain is suffering
        For there is no hope now.

He lifts the weighty weapon, lets it fall
Straight: the blade brushes the bare neck;   2310
But though the arm swung fiercely he felt no harm
For his neck was only nicked, a surface scratch;
Yet when the blade broke the fatty flesh
And bright blood shot over his shoulder to earth,
Seeing his own blood-spots mottle the snow,
He leapt forward, feet together, a spear-length,
Seized his helmet, and slammed it on his head;
With a heave of his shoulders he hastily swung his shield
In front of him, drew his sword and spoke out fiercely.
Not any morning since the one when his mother bore him   2320
Can he have been half so happy a man:

'Stop striking—now! Not one blow more!
I have received your stroke without strife or resistance.
If you give me more you'll get repaid:
It will be quick and fierce—you can count on what
          you've heard.
     Only one stroke will fall.
     That was our accord
     Last year in Arthur's hall.
     So stop. That was your word.'   2330

The man drew back. Upending his big weapon
He shoved the shaft into the ground, leaned over the blade
And studied the knight who stood there before him
In his fine armour, his fear of being harmed
Quite vanished. That sight warms the blood in his veins.
He pokes fun at him, cracks merry jokes
In a loud tone that rebounds off the stones:
'My good fellow, no need now to be so fierce!
In our fight no one has slighted you nor
Broken the conditions of our contract made at court.   2340
I promised one stroke only. You have handsomely paid
Your debt—you're freed from all other dues.
Perhaps I'd have struck you with much more power
Had I been nimbler, and hurt you horribly.
That first stroke was only a joke, a threat in jest;
I didn't hack you open, I hit you but lightly—rightly so
Because of our agreement fixed on that first evening
When you behaved well in my hall and gave me all
Your winnings as a wise and good man must.
And the second stroke I dealt you for that day   2350
When you kissed my wife and returned my rights to me.

[83]

(marginal annotations in handwriting: "not violence / not unharmed", "chivalry", "he kissed her - not adultery")

My arm missed both times: mere feints, no harm
    to show.
     Who pay their debts can rest
     Quite unafraid. And so,
     Because you failed the test
     Third time, you took that blow.

For that woven garment you wear is my own girdle.
My wife wove it,* so I know it well.
I have missed no facts concerning your acts and kisses,   2360
Nor my wife's wooing of you; I brought it all about.
I sent her to test you out. You withstood her stoutly.
You're the most faultless warrior who walks on foot!
As a pearl is more precious than a snow-pea
So is Gawain, upon my oath, among other knights.
Yet here you lacked a little: your loyalty
Was wanting—not out of greed, not out of wantonness,
But because you loved your life—and I blame you much less
For that.' Gawain stood still, his mind in pain,
So shaken with guilt, so grief-struck that he quaked within.   2370
The blood rushed from his heart, flushing his face.
He shrivelled in shame at what the bold man told him,
And the first words that he spoke were these:
'A curse upon my cowardice—and my covetousness!
There's villainy in both, and virtue-killing vice!'
He grasped the love-knot and loosened its clasp,
And hurled it hard in anger towards the man.
'There, take that tawdry love-token! Bad luck to it!
Craven fear of your blow, and cowardice, brought me
To give in to my greed and go against myself   2380
And the noble and generous code of knightly men.

I am proved false, faulty—those failings will haunt me.
From falsehood and faithlessness come a hollow heart and
ill-fame,*
And I confess to you
That I am much to blame.
What would you have me do
That I may cleanse my name?'

The lord laughed, and replied reasonably
And warmly: 'Any harm you've done is now undone.   2390
You've clearly confessed and freed yourself of fault.
You've paid your penance at the point of my blade;
I hold you absolved of all offence, and as fresh-made
As if, since birth, you had never sinned on earth.
And I give you back the girdle with the golden border.
It's green like my gown—so take it, Gawain,
To recall this contest when you ride away
Among proud princes, as an emblem to remember
Your quest and challenge at the Green Chapel. But the feast
Continues at my castle. Let us hurry home   2400
And resume our festival and our New Year revels
once more.
With my wife,' insisted the lord,
'Who was your foe before,
You'll find a new accord;
Of that I'm very sure.'

[handwritten: pride is a vice]

[handwritten: women have wiles]

But Gawain declines, catches hold of his helm
And politely puts it on, thanking the man most warmly:
'I have lingered long enough. Good luck to you,
And may He who bestows all honour show you His bounty.   2410

[85]

And commend me to your lovely lady, your courteous wife—
Both her and the other, my two honoured ladies,
Who so neatly tricked their knight with their nice ploy.
Yet it's no wonder if a fool's made mad
By the wiles of a woman, and suffers woe.
Adam in Paradise was thus deceived by one,
Solomon by more than one; Samson also—
Delilah sealed his fate—and, after that, David
Was betrayed and brought to sorrow by Bathsheba.*
Since these were gulled by their guiles, how fine it would be   2420
To love women warmly, yet believe no word that
They say. They were the noblest men we've known;
Fortune favoured them, they were the finest, the most blessed
          by Heaven.
          But by women they'd used
          Their wits were teased and riven.
          Now I, likewise abused,
          Perhaps will be forgiven.

'As for your girdle,' said Gawain, 'God reward you,
I shall bear it with the best will—not for its gleaming gold,   2430
Not for its fine-knotted cloth, nor its many pendants,
Not because of its cost or its handsome handiwork—
But I shall see it always, as a sign of my fault
Wherever I ride, remembering with remorse, in times of pride
How feeble is the flesh, how petty and perverse.
What a pestilent hutch and house of plagues it is,
Inviting filth!* And, if my vanity flare up,
When I see this love-lace it will humble me.
Now I would ask one thing, if you won't be offended:
Since you are lord of these lands where I have spent   2440

Many days in your friendship—may the One who reigns
High in Heaven reward you royally!—
By what name are you known? It's the last thing I'll ask.'
'Very well, I shall tell you,' the knight replied,
'By name I am known as Bertilak de Hautdesert.*
Through the power of Morgan le Fay, part of my menage—
By her wiles in witchcraft and her cleverness
She has mastered magic skills once kept by Merlin,
For it is well known that long ago she fell in love
With that wise wizard, as your knights have heard at your own
       hearth-side.   2451
     "Morgan the Goddess":* so
     Titled, since none can ride
     So tall, but with a blow
     She will cut down his pride—

'She had me to go in this guise to your hall
To test your mettle, gather whether there's truth
In the rumours of the Round Table's renown;
She worked this marvel on me to befuddle your brains
And cause Guinevere grief, kill her with fear   2460
Of a ghastly apparition that spoke like a ghoul
And twisted his head in his own hand at the High Table.
It is she who lives in my home, the hoary lady;
Arthur's half-sister, and your own aunt as well:
The Duchess of Tintagel's daughter, who bore,
Through union with Uther, the noble Arthur, now king.
So I beseech you, come back and greet your aunt
And celebrate in my hall. The whole house loves you.
And, as much as any man, I wish you well, for
The truth that you bear, and there's my oath on it.'   2470

Gawain again said, 'No—not by any means.'
They embraced and kissed, commending each other to Christ,
The Prince of Paradise, and parted right where
      they stood.
    Gawain tugged at the rein,
    Turned homeward fast as he could.
    And the knight in bright green
    Turned to wherever he would.*

And now Gawain rides along wild ways
On his good steed Gringolet, his life spared by grace.   2480
Sometimes he stayed in a dwelling, often out in the open;
He battled, and fought off vicious attacks in the valleys
Too many adventures to mention in this tale.
His neck-wound ceased to hurt him, slowly healed,
And he bore the green belt wound around him
Cross-wise as a baldric, bound fast to his side,
Its laces tied under his left arm* in a tassel,
Sign of the sorry fault that had found him out.
And thus, quite sound, the knight comes to the court.
When the king found Gawain come home, cries   2490
Of gratitude and great joy broke out, mounting as the king
And queen kissed him and all the court greeted him,
And all his trusted brother knights of the hall
Questioned him, marvelling as he told tales of the quest
And all the galling trials he had undergone:
The challenge at the Green Chapel, the antics of the man
In green, the loving friendship with the lady—and the girdle.
He bade them scan his bare neck for the scar,
That shameful hurt at the lord's hand, with himself
      to blame.   2500

> Grieving as he re-told
> The whole tale, his blood came
> Rushing, now hot, now cold,
> And his face flushed in shame.

'Look, my lord,' he said, touching the love-token.
'This band belongs with the wound I bear on my neck:
Sign of the harm I've done, and the hurt I've duly received
For covetousness and cowardice, for succumbing to deceit.
It is a token of untruth and I am trapped in it
And must wear it everywhere while my life lasts.
No one can hide, without disaster, a harmful deed.
What's done is done and cannot be undone.'
The king and the whole court comfort the knight,
Laughing loudly,* and they cordially decree
Right then, that lords and ladies of the Round Table
And all in their Brotherhood should wear a baldric
Bound cross-wise round them, a band of green
The same as sir Gawain's, to keep him company.
All agreed it was good for the Round Table's renown;
He who wore it would be honoured evermore,*
As it is recounted in the best books of old Romance.
These marvellous things took place in the age of Arthur
As the books of Britain, Brutus' isle, all tell.
Since Brutus, that bold man, first landed here
After the battle and the attack were over
>   at Troy,
> This land has often known
> Adventures like these. I pray
> That He of the thornèd crown
> Bring us all to His joy. *AMEN**

HONI SOYT QUI MAL PENSE*

[89]

EXPLANATORY NOTES

References to 'Brewer and Gibson' are to Derek Brewer and Jonathan Gibson, eds., *A Companion to the Gawain-poet* (Cambridge, 1997).

3   *That man enmeshed ... Aeneas, the high-born*: Aeneas, according to Classical legend, fled from the ruins of Troy to Italy to found what eventually became Rome. Various versions of the story behind the fall of Troy were current in the Middle Ages: the best known, told by Virgil in the *Aeneid*, presents Aeneas as a warrior-prince unfailingly loyal to the city; another, known through two supposedly eyewitness accounts of the Trojan War and retold by one of the best-known medieval historians of Troy, the thirteenth-century Guido delle Colonne, makes Aeneas complicit in its betrayal by Antenor. The language of the original text of *Gawain* leaves it obscure as to which version is being followed: it says that the man 'that the trammes of tresoun there wroght | Was tried for his trecherye, the truest on erthe'. This has various possible meanings, one being that given in this translation, another being that the man who wrought the treason (possibly Antenor) was marked out (*tried*) for his quintessential (*truest*) treachery. If the ambiguity of some of the words makes interpretation difficult, the lack of punctuation in medieval texts makes it impossible to be sure whether Aeneas is the man being referred to or not: the next line starts 'Hit was Ennias . . .', but this could be referring only forwards, to his conquests, rather than backwards to the treason as well.

all the wealth of the Western Isles: Aeneas's descendants supposedly continued the westwards imperial expansion begun by their forebear, giving their names to the lands they founded—as Langaberde to Lombardy. 'Ticius' is otherwise unknown.

Felix Brutus founds Britain: according to the inventive twelfth-century historian Geoffrey of Monmouth, Brutus was Aeneas's great-grandson, who went into voluntary exile after accidentally killing his father on a hunt with an arrow intended for a hart. 'Felix Brutus' means 'Brutus the blessed' or 'fortunate', an odd term to use in view of the story; it presumably refers to his founding of Britain, which according to folk etymology derived its name from him. Geoffrey also claims that he founded London, under the name of Troynovaunt, New Troy. There was a keen interest in this legendary history of the country at the time when the *Gawain*-poet was writing; one Londoner is reputed to have gone so far as to propose that the city be renamed 'Little Troy'. The 'French Sea' is the English Channel.

More marvels have occurred in this country: the promise of 'marvels' suggests the romance to follow. England, under its name of Logres, was supposed to have been particularly rich in marvels until the time of the end of the Grail quest—chronologically later in Arthur's reign, and therefore after the end of this particular story.

4 *I'll tell it to you now . . . As custom sets it down*: there is no evidence that the story did in fact exist before this poem was written, although some of its constituent motifs are certainly older (see Introduction, pp. xvii–xx). There was no particular cachet attaching to poetic originality in the Middle Ages: a well-tried story was to a new one what an antique is to factory-produced goods now. The poet is associating his work with the values attaching to antiquity even while creating something new. The 'interwoven letters' guaranteed by custom—'with lel letteres loken', locked with faithful letters, in the original—may be a further way of advertising the story as an ancient and stable text, or it may be a reference to the alliterative style itself, the interlocking letters that fix the words in place. The poet plays games with point of view throughout the poem, sometimes, as here, insisting that the poem is no more than a story that he has heard or read, at other times placing himself within the narrative as if he were present, or indeed within his protagonist's mind.

carol-dances: carol-dances were ring-dances, sometimes performed as an accompaniment to a song consisting of alternating refrains, sung by all the dancers as they moved, and stanzas, sung by a soloist and during which the dancers stood still.

fifteen long days: Christmas was traditionally celebrated with a twelve-day feast, from Christmas Day until 6 January; Arthur's fortnight-long feast is either an approximation or a luxury.

5 *Those seated at the dais*: the high table, reserved for the head of the household and the highest-ranking guests, was placed at the end of the hall where the floor was slightly raised (an arrangement still in operation at Oxford and Cambridge colleges). This was the normal medieval hall layout, but it is not the one traditionally associated with Arthur: the poet possibly avoids including the Round Table so as to make the Green Knight's entrance through the hall and between the side-tables to Arthur more impressive. It also means that the festivities at Camelot can be modelled on those of the king's court at Windsor.

Noel: the Anglo-French, and therefore the courtly, term for 'Christmas'.

Chaucer also describes people shouting 'Noel!' to greet the season in the *Franklin's Tale*.

5 *New Year gifts*: New Year, rather than Christmas, was the traditional time for gift-giving. Here, some kind of a game of forfeits seems to be at issue, in which the players have to guess what the presents are and either kiss or be kissed depending on whether or not they get the answer right; or the present-giving and the guessing-games may refer to different pastimes.

When they had washed: a ceremonial washing of the hands before, and often after, a meal was a standard part of the ceremony of fine eating, basins, ewers, and towels being brought by squires for the purpose.

Toulouse . . . Turkestan: the names are probably meant to indicate exoticism rather than exact locations. The 'tars' of the original can be loosely interpreted to cover Turkestan, Turkey, and the biblical Tharsia —all places in the Orient such as could be associated with the silk trade.

grey eyes: grey eyes were considered the acme of beauty in the Middle Ages; the term may overlap with what we would now call blue eyes.

6 *never to eat at feasts . . . splendid adventure*: Arthur's refusal to eat at a major feast, either Christmas or Pentecost, before some adventure or marvel happens, is a common opening to Arthurian stories. What he is expecting on this occasion, however—an exciting story or a chivalric challenge—falls far short of what actually happens.

Gawain . . . Agravain . . . Baldwin . . . Iwain, Urien's son: the names are all those of figures familiar in Arthurian romance. Gawain and Agravain were the sons of Arthur's half-sister, who was born to his mother by her first husband, the Duke of Tintagel; Uther Pendragon, Arthur's father, was her second husband. As Arthur's eldest nephew at the feast, Gawain has pride of place beside the Queen. She is in the centre, to the left of Arthur's chair; on its right, in the place of honour, is Bishop Baldwin, the highest-ranking ecclesiastic present, with Iwain beside him. In the French prose romances, Iwain is also Arthur's nephew by another half-sister, Morgan le Fay; she is to be important in the poem later, but not because of her relationship to Iwain.

7 *Each pair has twelve full dishes*: two people were the unit of service in medieval feasts: they might also share a single cup and plate, especially at less luxurious meals, or at the lower tables. Twelve dishes is the distinguishing mark of a major feast. The announcing of each new course with trumpets and kettledrums was common at feasts.

astride his horse: a high-ranking guest might be invited to ride his horse into a castle courtyard without dismounting at the gate, as Gawain does later; but riding into the hall would be an act either of hostility, or of discourtesy arising from insolence or ignorance (the latter exemplified by the rustic Perceval when he first comes to Arthur's court), or of entertainment of a kind commonly offered between the courses of a major feast: after the Green Knight has left, Arthur compares his visit to just such an interlude. The 'King's champion' also entered the hall on horseback at a coronation feast to challenge anyone who did not accept the king's right to rule, but that is relevant here only in so far as it conveys the potential hostility of a mounted man among the feasters. In Chaucer's *Squire's Tale*, a strange knight enters the hall on a horse of brass, in a passage possibly influenced by *Gawain*.

8   *he was bright green . . . the man and his garments as well*: 'green knights', in the sense of knights who wear green surcoats and perhaps green-painted armour, and who ride horses in green trappings, are widespread in romances; to have a knight who is himself green, riding a green horse, is a different phenomenon altogether. The meaning of the knight's greenness has been much debated (see Introduction, p. xxix); perhaps the key point about it is that it is simply inexplicable. The word *fade*, here translated as 'colossal', mentioned just before the greenness, never occurs elsewhere, so the meaning has to be guessed at: alternatives include 'hostile', 'bold', and 'like a fairy or demon'.

    stockinged feet: the original reads 'scholes', which might refer to a form of shoes, or mean 'shoeless'. Hose with leather reinforcements under the sole in place of shoes were fashionable in the fifteenth century, and may be indicated by an illustration in the early fourteenth-century Luttrell Psalter; they were not for heavy-duty wear, and would maintain the ambiguity of the Green Knight between martial threat and courtliness.

9   *like a king's cape*: an example of the kind of thing the poet has in mind can be seen attached to the helmet on the near-contemporary effigy of the Black Prince in Canterbury Cathedral.

10   *holly . . . when all the groves are leafless*: this line is invariably cited by those who believe that the Green Knight represents the relic of a vegetation myth, or at least the death and renewal of life at the New Year, but other interpretations are also possible. Green branches could be carried as a sign of peace (as the Green Knight himself points out later), and holly is one of the few available at New Year; it was also metonymically associated with winter. The rival meanings suggested by the holly (peace) and the axe (war) are typical of the poet's determination to keep the Green Knight's significance undefinable.

    Where is . . . The leader of this lot?: Arthur is out of his place at the High Table, so cannot be immediately located—though since he would presumably be wearing his crown at such a high feast, the Green

Knight clearly does not take the trouble to look far. The degree of insolence in the Green Knight's language is hard to gauge through the poet's dialect, but he is certainly not going out of his way to be polite.

12 *to strike one stroke for another*: many premodern games, from tournaments to football, commonly resulted in death or injury; but a 'diversion for the New Year' that consists of chopping off your opponent's head unites pastime and violence in quite bizarre fashion. On the motif of the return blow in other romances, see the Introduction, p. xviii.

13 *Arthur's house . . . Whose fame flies through the remotest regions*: the earlier emphasis on the youth and newness of the court means that its fame does not yet have the backing of all the later Arthurian adventures to give it substance. In a shame culture, which measures worth in terms of reputation, the suggestion that a reputation is unjustified amounts to saying that the society is worthless.

15 *Please, my good liege . . . without blame, decree*: Gawain's speech, in contrast to the Green Knight's, is conspicuously courteous and self-deprecating, in keeping with his English reputation as the model of courtesy. Every detail of it—asking permission to leave the queen's side, the offer to give counsel to the king (since it was a mark of good kingship to listen to advice, Gawain is in effect asserting Arthur's excellence as a ruler), the implied rebuke to the Green Knight, the insistence on the knights' courage and fierceness and their own skill in counsel—is designed to restore the court's self-respect. He is careful, too, not to let it appear that he is in any way special for taking on the challenge. His reminder that he is Arthur's nephew is none the less a way of enhancing his standing in the Green Knight's eyes, and no one, whether court onlooker or reader, is in practice going to underestimate his courage.

Let's repeat our agreement before we go further: the agreement begins to take on the qualities not only of a pledged word but of a formal contract, which in the Middle Ages was not required to be written in order to be binding. Gawain is being asked to confirm the small print—he will not be able to find his way out on a technicality.

teach me | Your true name, that I may trust you: 'By the name one knows the man', the young Perceval is told in the *Conte del Graal* of Chrétien de Troyes. Questing knights often concealed their identities; Gawain is exceptionally forthcoming in acknowledging his own. The Green Knight's desire to 'trust' Gawain through his 'true' name is reciprocated by Gawain's response 'In good faith': faithfulness and truth are to be the key themes of what follows.

18 *the noblest at the table*: the original reads 'the derrest on the dece', 'the most worthy on the dais', which could refer to the nobles generally, or to Guinevere alone—in which case this would be the only line to offer any support to the Green Knight's later claim that the object of the whole exercise was to scare Guinevere to death.

you cannot fail to find me . . . craven coward: knights on quests in romances almost always do find what they seek, but they set out without knowing whether they will do so or not; the only person, or personification, that one cannot fail to find is Death. The formulation is therefore particularly threatening, although the poet stops short of making the identification precise (just as all his other hints as to what the Green Knight might symbolize remain unconfirmed). Gawain is at once given a strong reason why he should act like a craven coward, and reminded of what the consequences of such an action would be: to be known as such would destroy the whole basis of his knightly reputation and show him to be worthless.

Laughed as they watched him go: laughter can signify many things in the Middle Ages: most often happiness or festive merriment, sometimes mockery. Sheer relief of a slightly hysterical kind is no doubt part of the reaction here.

interludes: pageants and entertainments between courses were a feature of luxurious feasts, and often included elaborate disguisings, stage properties such as ships or castles, or animals. The wedding celebrations for Margaret of York in 1468 included a lion that walked around the hall opening and closing its mouth and singing a two-part song (tenor and treble); the need for hearing the words presumably meant that the parts were taken by singers at the side, not by the front and back legs (*Mémoires d'Olivier de la Marche*, ed. H. Beaune and J. d'Arbaumont (Paris, 1883–8), iii. 135). Just as the horse in *Gawain* is a real horse, though green, Arthur does not claim that what has happened *is* an interlude, just that it can be compared to one.

19 *hang up your axe*: the phrase was a proverbial one, meaning that business was over. Arthur is punning on the literal meaning of the phrase.

20 *Our endings rarely square with our beginnings*: the aphorism expresses a commonplace, but may be based on the *Distichs*, a series of maxims in Latin couplets wrongly ascribed to Cato and widely known in the Middle Ages.

the year followed fast behind: the description of the seasons that follows fills in the period between New Year and Gawain's setting out. Descriptions of spring are widespread in romances; that these verses include not only the growth of new life in spring but the 'dwindling' of the year into autumn and winter is a reminder that more is going on in this story than the idyllic glamour of youth, love, and chivalry found in other romance texts. There are other descriptions of all the seasons in medieval literature—one that was particularly widely known appears as part of Aristotle's instruction of the young Alexander in the *Secretum Secretorum*—but they rarely achieve the energy, dynamism, and sharpness of observation given by the *Gawain*-poet.

20 *Lent . . . simple fare*: Lent, the six weeks before Easter, was a period of fasting, when meat was forbidden; fish was, however, allowed, as in modern Roman Catholic practice.

21 *the Michaelmas moon*: Michaelmas, the feast of St Michael, falls on 29 September, and was the day on which debts were called in and wages and rents paid—a suggestive time for Gawain to begin to think of receiving his own repayment. It is close to the autumn equinox, when the nearest full moon is particularly conspicuous: the more recent term is the harvest moon. All Hallows' Day, or All Saints' Day, when Gawain declares that he must set out, is 1 November; he leaves the next day, which is All Souls' Day, the day of commemoration of all the dead.

22 *Iwain and Erik . . . Lancelot . . . Mador de la Port*: many of the names would have been more familiar from French Arthurian romances than English. Before Malory compiled the *Morte Darthur* in the 1460s, Lancelot never enjoyed the kind of popularity in England that he had in France. Gawain is most likely to be the protagonist of English Arthurian romances; if he is not actually the central character, he is likely to be the knight by whom the prowess of the other knights is measured.

We must engage our fate: the romance imperative of the quest, to take the adventure that shall fall to you.

Calls early for his arms: the 'arming of the hero' is one of the great setpieces of many epics and romances. It was sufficiently familiar for Chaucer to parody it in his own Canterbury tale, *Sir Thopas*, in which the ritual starts with Sir Thopas's underpants. Since the various items that comprised the armour overlapped downwards, they were put on, as described here, from the feet upwards. Gawain's armour combines the luxurious and the practical: he will be a battle machine, but a very handsome one. Fashions in armour changed steadily over the Middle Ages: Gawain's is distinctively of the late fourteenth century. See further Michael Lacy, 'Armour I', Brewer and Gibson, 166–73.

23 *Girt with a silken band*: the 'silk saynt', the silken girdle that supports Gawain's sword, emblem of his knighthood, is marked as being of particular significance only by its placing at the end of the wheel; it is

one of the details to be registered as important only on a second reading, when the story of the second silken girdle is known.

he goes to hear Mass: daily attendance at Mass, whenever possible, was a required element of late medieval piety. Attendance before a journey was particularly important in invoking God's blessing on the day ahead, and in preparing one's soul in the case of death.

Gringolet: Gawain's winning of Gringolet from an opponent is recounted in the French Arthurian romances. Exceptional horses are occasionally named in romance, the most famous being the Bayard of Renaud of Montauban (the Italian Rinaldo).

24   *quickly kisses it*: compare the priest's kissing of the stole at his robing, signifying his acceptance of the yoke of Christ; the kissing of the helmet perhaps indicates acceptance of chivalric, including Christian, duty. According to a handbook of chivalry widely known across Europe, written by Ramon Lull and eventually translated by Caxton, *The Book of the Ordre of Chivalry* (ed. A. T. P. Byles, Early English Text Society OS 168 (1926)), the helmet signifies humility or dread of shame.

the shield . . . And its pentangle: the intricate detail of the symbolism of Gawain's heraldic device is exceptional both in historical heraldry and in fiction. The pentangle has the advantage of being free of ready-made or generally established symbolism: while medieval parallels can be found, one has to look a long way for them. The poet can therefore impose his own connotations on the number so strongly as to override any familiar numerological associations. The first quality that he stresses about the pentangle is that it is an 'endless knot', a five-pointed star (as distinct from a pentagon, a five-sided figure), such as can be drawn without taking the pencil off the paper: break it, and one is left with nothing but a piece of string, something like a lace, or a girdle. In its unbroken form, the figure represents wholeness, perfection. Mathematically, it carries a relationship to the perfect proportion known now (but not in the Middle Ages) as the Golden Section —whether the poet knew of its mathematical possibilities is however another matter, and certainly not necessary so far as the poem is concerned.

a design that Solomon devised: 'Solomon's knot' was a term that could be used for any densely interwoven pattern. The modern usage of 'Solomon's seal' denotes the star of David, a six-pointed star consisting of two superimposed equilateral triangles (and not therefore an 'unending knot'). Solomon was famous for his wisdom, which in the Middle Ages was sometimes taken as having a supernatural edge to it—learning overlapped with the arts of magic, as Sir Bertilak notes later of Morgan.

token of truth: compare the description of the silken girdle as a 'token of untruth' at the end of the poem. 'Truth' is the central concept that subsumes all the five sets of five virtues; see Introduction, pp. xxix–xxx.

25 *his five senses*: sight, hearing, touch, taste, and smell.

the five wounds . . . as the Creed tells: the five wounds suffered by Christ at the Crucifixion are the marks of the nails in His hands and feet, and the wound of the spear in His side. The Creed—so called from its first word, *credo*, 'I believe'—summarizes essential Christian doctrine.

the five joys . . . from her child: devotion to the Virgin Mary emerged as a major element of piety in the earlier Middle Ages, producing such titles as 'Queen of Heaven'; the coronation of the Virgin in Heaven by God became widespread as an artistic theme. Her 'five joys' were most often enumerated as those of Luke 1–2, the Annunciation, the Visitation to Elisabeth, the Nativity, the Presentation in the Temple, and the Finding in the Temple. Alternative lists sometimes incorporate the Epiphany (the coming of the Magi), the Resurrection, and the Assumption (the doctrine of the bodily assumption of the Virgin into Heaven, which was made orthodox dogma only as recently as 1950). According to Geoffrey of Monmouth, who was largely responsible for creating the legendary history of Arthur, it was Arthur rather than Gawain who carried the Virgin's image painted inside his shield.

generosity, good fellowship, | Cleanness . . . courtesy . . . compassion: generosity ('fraunchyse') implied nobleness of spirit as well as open-handedness. 'Good fellowship' included faithfulness in friendship and a sense of duty as the member of a group as well as good companionship. 'Cleanness' primarily indicates sexual purity, though the *Gawain*-poet's own poem on the subject extends its meaning to spiritual uprightness too; in its sexual sense it is somewhat surprising to find as an attribute of Gawain—in the French romances (though rarely in English) he is often presented as making advances to the ladies he meets, and is therefore contrasted with celibate knights such as Galahad or faithful lovers such as Lancelot. 'Courtesy' is a matter not just of good manners, but of inward as well as outward concern for others. 'Pité', rendered here as 'compassion', has a semantic range at this period from pity to piety: piety as the performing of one's religious duties includes care towards others.

red gold on red gules: 'red' was the commonest medieval adjective for the colour of gold. The rules of heraldry required that metals (gold or silver) were set on colours (such as red): one colour, or one metal, could not be superimposed on another.

26 *Logres*: a Celtic-derived term for England, 'England' itself being anachronistic as a name in an Arthurian story set before the coming of

the Angles. As the opening stanza shows, the poet is alert to national etymology.

27   *the wastes of Northern Wales . . . Wirral, the wilderness*: Wales, apart from the anglicized towns, was considered an alien and dangerous place by most medieval Englishmen. Gawain's journey takes him along the coast of North Wales to the mouth of the Dee. 'Holyhead' cannot be the town of that name on the far tip of Anglesey, since it clearly indicates a place at which a crossing of the estuary into Cheshire was possible; the Holy Well of St Winifred in Flintshire seems most likely, though it is not actually on the coast. The Wirral was notorious as a refuge for outlaws, though the comment here on the wildness of its inhabitants could also be a joke against the poem's first readers since Gawain is travelling into their own home territory. This is, however, the dangerous past, not the familiar present.

with dragons, or with wolves . . . And giants from the high fells: this is very much a romance landscape, in contrast to the 'worse' winter that is described next. Dragons and giants were thoroughly familiar as the standard material of romances, though it is standard material in which the poet has singularly little interest. The wodwos, wild men, were typically imagined as being covered with thick hair and armed with clubs. Bears had long been extinct in Britain, and wolves probably for some centuries. Wild cattle (which were white in colour) are recorded around London in the twelfth century, though the population had been fragmented by the *Gawain*-poet's time; a herd still survives at Chillingham in Northumberland. One of the legendary exploits of the hero Guy of Warwick was the killing of a particularly fierce wild cow (less impressive than Gawain's bulls). The 'savage boars' were likewise a possibility—see note to p. 52 below—but they too frequented romances rather more liberally than Britain by the late fourteenth century. (See James Edmund Harting, *British Animals Extinct within Historic Times* (London, 1880).)

28   *he rides on merrily*: compare 'Tell your sorrows to your saddle-bow, and ride singing forth' (a proverb ascribed in the twelfth century to King Alfred, quoted by Derek Brewer, 'Introduction', Brewer and Gibson, 9).

Never see the Lord's service . . . to assuage our sorrow: Gawain is anxious to find a place where he can hear a Mass for Christmas; Christ 'assuages sorrow' through redeeming mankind from sin and death.

29   *Paternoster, Ave and Creed*: the Lord's Prayer, 'Hail Mary', and Creed were the basic toolkit of piety for the lay Christian.
Saint Julian: the patron saint of hospitality.

30   *double ditch*: possibly two ditches, but perhaps more likely a

Explanatory Notes

double-width moat such as required the earth dug out to be thrown twice—once from the centre outwards, and again to the edge (Michael Thompson, 'Castles', Brewer and Gibson, 125).

30 *a model made from paper*: such paper models, sometimes gilded, were used to decorate dishes at elaborate feasts; the *Gawain*-poet makes another reference to them in his description of Belshazzar's feast in *Cleanness*. Chaucer's rather puritanical Parson was scathing about them, citing them as an example of 'pride of the table' (*Canterbury Tales*, x. 445).

by Saint Peter . . . replied the porter: the porter is the gatekeeper; his oath fits him since St Peter keeps the gates of heaven.

31 *to receive the knight properly*: the next few lines describe this 'proper' reception; hospitality was a virtue expected of landowners, and the reception accorded to guests would be carefully graded. The servants kneel to Gawain in honour of his rank; instead of being required to dismount and enter through a wicket-gate, the great gates themselves are opened so that he can ride into the courtyard. While the servants take Gringolet to be stabled, the higher-ranking knights and squires escort him inside to where the lord of the castle meets him. On the rituals of hospitality, see Felicity Heal, *Hospitality in Early Modern England* (Oxford, 1990), 1–36.

32 *regal bedding . . . curtains . . . carpets . . . covered the floor*: textiles, including hangings and bed-curtains, were commonly the second highest item of expenditure after food in a well-to-do household. Carpets would be an exceptional luxury; they probably indicate textiles laid down for a guest (rather as a cloth is laid for Gawain's armour) rather than fixed features of the room. They were first used in England by Queen Eleanor of Castile in the mid-thirteenth century, to the disgust of the Londoners; as late as the 1470s they were still a subject for remark, along with the white silk hangings that covered the walls in the 'chambers of pleasance' set up for the visit to Edward IV's court of a guest to whom Edward owed particular gratitude (see John Gloag, *A Short Dictionary of Furniture* (rev. edn., London, 1969), 36, and Margaret Wood, *The English Mediaeval House* (London, 1965), 393).

33 *dishes of various fish*: Christmas Eve, as the final day of the penitential season of Advent, is a fast day; Gawain politely declares that the food is as good as a feast.

34 *The subtle speech of love*: the reputation of the French Gawain as lover and ladies' man here begins to intrude on the English Gawain's more innocuous, and gender-inclusive, courtesy.

36 *The other . . . buttocks full and wide*: descriptions of hideous old women were a formal rhetorical set-piece, also found, for instance, in the Old

Woman of the French *Romance of the Rose* (a text known to the *Gawain*-poet) and the hag of Chaucer's *Wife of Bath's Tale* and its various analogues. Chaucer's hag has supernatural associations, and it may be that the ugliness of the old woman here would suggest to a medieval audience that there is similarly more to her than meets the eye. The beauty of the younger woman is described in less physical detail, but, much more tellingly, by the impression she makes on Gawain.

spices: commonly served with wine in rich households after the evening meal, rather like coffee and chocolates.

He snatched his hood off: hoods are mentioned in several texts, including *Piers Plowman*, as barter or prizes in games.

37 *St John's Day*: 27 December; the three days of hunting that immediately precede New Year's Day must occupy 29, 30, and 31 December, leaving one day unaccounted for. A line may have dropped out of the poem in the copying, or the poet may simply have elided the extra day since it served no narrative purpose.

40 *For hunting in the wood*: hunting was one of the most renowned of aristocratic pastimes, enjoyed by every monarch down to the seventeenth century. It had its own elaborate terminology and rituals, which are followed in meticulous detail in the accounts of the lord's own hunts.

Whatever I win . . . whatever you earn: the phrasing is financial and commercial. The poet has a particular alertness to the way in which earlier non-monetary concepts of worth and value—in terms of social hierarchy, prowess, or virtue—were being infiltrated by the assumptions of a cash economy. There is an economics of knighthood being set up here that would have been hard to produce before the fourteenth century. The exchange also subtly insists—though Gawain is in no position to see it at this moment—that the hunt involves him more closely than he might think: ultimately, it is his life that is being bartered for, and pursued. (See Jill Mann, 'Price and Value in *Sir Gawain and the Green Knight*', *Essays in Criticism*, 36 (1986), 294–328.)

41 *French phrases . . . light douceurs*: French language and manners, with possible further associations of the sweet-talking of women, are suggestive of the highest social levels: this may be a provincial court geographically, but not in behaviour.

42 *Straight after Mass . . . hastily*: there was an abbreviated form of the Mass for people in a hurry, known as the *missa venatoria*, a hunting mass. The 'light meal' is specified in the original as a 'sop', bread

dipped in wine, probably eaten standing.

42 *terrified deer raced through the dale*: what follows is the account of a deer-drive, a hunt of barren female deer rather than the pursuit of a single stag. The detail can be abundantly confirmed from a number of medieval hunting manuals, including the most famous, the near-contemporary *Livre de Chasse* of Gaston Phébus, count of Foix (see chapter 36 of its early fifteenth-century translation by Edward, Duke of York, edited as *The Master of Game* by W. A. and F. Baillie-Grohman (London, 1909)). Hinds and does did not rank as the noblest of beasts to hunt, being classed as 'beasts of chase' rather than 'beasts of venery'. Deer-drives are also described in two other late medieval Northern poems, *The Awntyrs* [adventures] *of Arthur at the Tarn Wathelin*, and *Summer Sunday*. On hunting, see Anne Rooney, *Hunting in Middle English Literature* (Cambridge, 1993).

43 *galloped, and dismounted*: the lord gallops to chase the does, dismounts to shoot at them.

while the light streams down his walls: the sun is near the winter solstice and therefore at its lowest, so shines through the window onto the walls rather than the floor.

45 *more fitting clothes*: it was normal practice to sleep naked.

To serve you at your leisure: the words stop short of being downright sexual invitation, but not very far short. Gawain is careful to take 'service' solely in a chivalric sense.

46 *Mary reward you*: commonplace as such phrases are, their accumulation in Gawain's addresses to the lady begins to have the quality of an exorcism, of prayers to keep her at bay. Mary, exemplar of sexual purity, is especially appropriate for such purposes, as is made explicit when she keeps an eye on her knight on the lady's third visit.

47 *Were she the brightest beauty . . . forestall*: the original text shows a confusion of syntax at this point, compounded by the customary absence of punctuation. It is not clear whether the thoughts are the narrator's, or Gawain's, or even the lady's, or where one set might stop and another start; the first line as given in the manuscript reads 'I' for 'she' and 'lady' for 'knight'. The emendations adopted here are the most elegant, and in many ways the simplest, solution.

it's hard to be sure you're really sir Gawain: Gawain's concern with his reputation in the eyes of the world has been abundantly demonstrated by the pentangle; now, the lady challenges him to live up to a very different kind of reputation (see Introduction, pp. xix–xx).

48 *chamberlain*: as the term implies, the chamberlain is the servant in charge of the chamber, the private room as distinct from the public hall.

as custom demands: the breaking of the deer was as meticulously prescribed as the rules of the hunt, and the poet follows the prescriptions precisely, down to the serving to the dogs of the offal mixed with bread on the deerskin. Besides the accounts in the hunting manuals, there are closely comparable accounts of the breaking of a deer in the alliterative *Parliament of the Three Ages* and in the romance of *Sir Tristrem*—Sir Tristram supposedly being the instigator and supreme master of the rituals of the hunt. The mixture of destructive violence and finely observed courtly ritual repeats in the lord the duality of meaning already established for the Green Knight.

51   *The rooster . . . crowed three times*: cocks start crowing from well before dawn, and one could normally expect to let several dozen crows pass before rising, especially on a long winter night. Timing one's rising by the rooster was a commonplace of medieval life: mechanical clocks were still very rare in the poet's time.

52   *the most marvellous boar*: the poet builds up the energy of the hunt for over twenty lines before he identifies the quarry. As a 'beast of venery', the boar is the most noble beast to be hunted in the poem. Boar-hunts were the most dangerous kind: as Gaston Phébus pointed out, a boar could kill with a single stroke of his tusks. Boar-hunts figure in all the hunting manuals, and in many romances, but fully wild swine were becoming unusual in England by this date and may have been virtually extinct outside the parks that functioned as game preserves. They had been common in the hills around London in the twelfth century; the last major population in the south, in the Forest of Dean, never recovered from Henry III's order of two hundred for his Christmas feast of 1251 (at which they supplemented an order for over eight hundred assorted deer). There is a legend that the last wild boar in England was killed on Wild Boar Fell in Westmorland by Sir Richard de Musgrave, close to the date of composition of the poem. The story receives some confirmation from the fact that when his tomb in Kirkby Stephen church was opened in 1847, a boar-tusk was found with the skeleton. It is hard to be sure of the final extinction date of fully wild boars, however, not least as those kept in parks escaped from time to time and caused mayhem in the surrounding countryside. They seem to have died out even within parks in the course of the seventeenth century. See further Harting, *British Animals*, 77–114, supplemented by Oliver Rackham, *Ancient Woodland: Its History, Vegetation and Uses in England* (London, 1980), 181, and J. F. Hodgson, 'Kirkby Stephen Church', *Transactions of the Cumberland and Westmorland Antiquarian and Archaeological Society*, 4 (1880), 178–249.

loner, cut off from his kind: the French word for boar, *sanglier*, was derived from the habit of mature boars of separating themselves from the rest of the herd and living single. For 'kind', the poet uses the correct collective noun for wild swine (of both sexes), 'sounder': a herd of deer; a pride of lions; a sounder of swine; an exaltation of larks. The collective term for (male) boars is a 'singular': its perversity as a plural may make two points, that boars are not often found collectively, and that it would be a singular experience if one did. Many of the rich mine of collective nouns originated in hunting terminology; there is a fine collection of them in the late fifteenth-century hunting manual known as *The Book of St Albans*.

52   *destroyed three dogs*: boar-hunts regularly exacted a high price in the lives of hunting-dogs; the beast's grunting, as the manuals note, was a sign of particular danger. Shooting arrows at the animal was a recommended way of weakening it before the hunters went in for the kill, even though its hide was too tough to be pierced.

55   *the text and the very title of those volumes*: the lady's choice of phrase turns 'deeds of love and war' into romances in front of our eyes—or perhaps into rather ambiguous handbooks of chivalric behaviour.

57   *Unsheathes a bright sword*: this is either extremely heroic, or extremely foolhardy, or both. The correct weapon for killing a boar was the boar-spear, its length ensuring that the impaled boar died before it could reach the hunter. Swords figure in some romances as the weapons used in killing boars, but usually only when the hero is caught unprepared.

58   *The boar's head*: this was the part of the animal used for ceremonial presentation, as traditionally happened at the Christmas feast at the Queen's College, Oxford (a northern foundation), where it was carried into the hall to the accompaniment of the 'Boar's Head Carol'. The lord likewise presents the 'huge head' to Gawain—perhaps as part of the softening-up process of a man due to be beheaded himself two days later. The Queen's custom supposedly originated when a student found himself face to jaws with a boar outside Oxford, and shoved the volume of Aristotle that he was carrying down its throat.

59   *By Saint Giles!*: St Giles had associations with travellers and hunters. According to legend, he was crippled by an arrow while protecting a hind from huntsmen. Another legend has Charlemagne come to him for absolution for a sin he did not dare to confess, but the sin was revealed to Giles by an angel. Any or all of these associations might be suggestive for *Sir Gawain*, but the saint's great popularity in the Middle Ages might be sufficient explanation for the oath.

61   *the fox lay lurking*: the fox is the last, and the least noble, of the beasts hunted; it was usually classed as a beast of chase, but could be regarded as vermin (as vixens most often were) and trapped rather than hunted.

It may be the rarity of medieval accounts of fox-hunting (Layamon's *Brut*, of the early thirteenth century, contains almost the only English example) that leaves space for the poet here to describe the hunt much more from the point of view of the animal than the hunters.

62 *Reynard*: this is the personal name given to the fox in French fables and beast-epics (and in Chaucer's *Nun's Priest's Tale*), as well as being the common noun (*renard*).

she throws wide the window: presumably a glazed casement window rather than a shutter closing an unglazed aperture, since the light has previously been described as streaming in. Such windows were still very unusual (they are first heard of in England in an order for a royal palace a century earlier, but are otherwise hard to document before the fifteenth century), and again indicate the luxury and attention to the latest architectural technology of the household. (See Wood, *English Mediaeval House*, 352.)

64 *by St John*: St John the Apostle was a male parallel to the Virgin Mary in his sexual purity.

65 *a ring . . . a fine fortune*: the cash value of the ring makes it impossible for Gawain to reciprocate in a process of gift exchange; its symbolism as a love-token, which rings commonly represented, similarly rules out reciprocation on his part.

66 *And besought him . . . He conceded*: there would not be any point in taking the girdle if Gawain intended to part with it; but his malfeasance is underlined by his giving his word to the lady that he will not reveal it, so committing himself to breaking his word to the lord to hand over his winnings.

67 *He absolved him completely . . . Judgement Day*: Gawain goes to confession in preparation for the death he expects the next day; but the absolution he is given cannot in fact be complete, since he has pledged himself to breaking his word, and absolution cannot be given for a sin he is still intending to commit. The implication of the line may be that having concealed the girdle physically, he has buried the idea of it too.

He has finished off the fox he'd followed so long: the perfect tense of the verb—'he *has finished*'—may be proleptic, anticipating the death of the fox that follows; or it may refer to the other prey, Gawain himself, who has been covertly hunted over the three days.

68 *stripped of his tawny coat*: there were no rituals for the death of a fox other than the calls on the hunting-horns to mark the completion of the hunt. The tawdriness of the lord's half of the exchange of winnings with Gawain will match the imperfect reciprocation that Gawain makes.

72   *metal rings rubbed clean of rust*: chain mail was polished by rolling it in a barrel of sand.

73   *He wound his love-token twice around him*: Gawain bears the girdle both literally and metaphorically on top of his own badge—the pentangle on his coat-armour.

75   *Hector's*: Hector was the greatest of the Trojan heroes. He shares with Arthur the distinction of being listed among the Nine Worthies, the nine men of most prowess in the medieval view of world history.

    however skilled at arms . . . or any other man: the knight, priest, and churl are the representatives of the three estates that make up society (those who fight, those who pray, and those who labour). That the Green Knight kills them all reinforces the suggestion in his words to Gawain at Camelot that he is a figure of Death.

77   *gallops off and away, leaving Gawain | Still there*: who or what is the guide? If he is telling the truth about the Green Chapel, then the primary form of the shape-shifting Bertilak must be as the Green Knight; but in that case, the castle from which the guide comes, and to which he returns, would not be as safe or as solid a construct as he seems to think. If, alternatively, he is consciously lying, it must be because he has inside knowledge of Bertilak's schemes. He is a figure somewhat like the Third Murderer in *Macbeth*, not quite explicable in any terms.

    a barrow: generally taken in its current sense, to indicate an ancient burial-mound; they often had superstitious associations. The chamber in the centre would normally be closed up with earth, but here Gawain seems to be able to look inside it. The term can alternatively indicate any sort of rounded hill. The particularity of the scenery has encouraged attempts to locate the actual site of the Green Chapel. Ralph Elliott favours Ludchurch, 'a stupendous cleft of some 100 yards in length, from 30 to 40 feet in depth, and with a breadth ranging from six to ten feet' ('Landscape and Geography', Brewer and Gibson, 116) in a hill of considerable size. The place is undoubtedly spooky, and in the right area for the poet's dialect, but whether the mound or the crevice described in the poem amounts to anything so colossal is open to question. In any case, the belief in an actual site may be misplaced: a murderous shape-shifter is not likely to inhabit anywhere that can be visited casually by modern—or medieval—tourists.

78   *green gown . . . to destroy me*: in Chaucer's *Friar's Tale*, the devil wears green.

79   *mill-water | In a race*: watermills were much the commonest kind of mill. Needing a fast-flowing head of water to turn the wheel, they were

correspondingly dangerous: a number of the miracles ascribed to Henry VI after his death involved children who had apparently drowned after falling into mill-races (Ronald A. Knox, *The Miracles of King Henry VI* (London, 1923)).

81 *You're not Gawain . . . so good*: just as the lady had challenged Gawain on the grounds of his amatory reputation, the Green Knight taunts him with not living up to his chivalric reputation.

84 *woven garment . . . My wife wove it*: it may not be coincidence that 'weaving' is the verb also used for plots and spells, and that weaving is traditionally a woman's occupation.

85 *I am proved false . . . ill fame*: the Green Knight sees how close Gawain has come to perfection; Gawain sees how far he has fallen short. If he can't be the perfect man, he will cast himself as the worst of sinners.

86 *the wiles of a woman . . . by Bathsheba*: the retreat into the formulae of misogyny indicates an awareness on the part of the poet that the idealized phraseology of courtly love is the flip side of antifeminism. It was common practice to blame Eve for the Fall of Man. Solomon had three hundred wives and seven hundred concubines and complained that he had never found a good woman; David spied on Bathsheba as she bathed, seduced her, and then arranged the murder of her husband —neither story necessarily supporting the moral Gawain reads into it, though he was by no means alone in the Middle Ages in doing so. He is justifying himself, both by blaming the conventional scapegoat, and by aligning himself with the greatest biblical heroes, 'the noblest men we've known'. See further *Woman Defamed and Woman Defended: An Anthology of Medieval Texts*, ed. Alcuin Blamires (Oxford, 1992).

How feeble is the flesh . . . Inviting filth: in a traditional triplet, the flesh was associated with the temptations of the world and the devil in inviting men to sin.

87 *Bertilak de Hautdesert*: the name is sometimes transcribed as Bercilak, since the forms for -c- and -t- can be so close as to be indistinguishable; but a Berthelai figures in French romance (in the prose *Lancelot* in particular) and is anglicized as Bertilak in the fifteenth-century translation of the French *Merlin*. It would seem likely that the name was inspired by the poet's own French reading. The Berthelai of *Lancelot* is an old knight who plots against Arthur by declaring that Guinevere is an impostor, and is burned when his guilt is revealed; the stories are so different as to rule out any possibility that the *Gawain*-poet intended his Bertilak to represent the same character (see the summary by Corin Corley in his translation of *Lancelot of the Lake* (Oxford, 1989), 415–17). 'Hautdesert' can be translated as 'high wilderness'; it has been

compared to the High Peak in the *Gawain* area of the Pennines, called 'Autepeek' or 'Haute Peek' in the fourteenth century. Both parts of the name are discussed by Brewer, 'Some Names', Brewer and Gibson, 192–4. The revelation of the name might be expected to explain everything: in fact, we, and Gawain, know no more with the name than without it. The one character in the story to remain anonymous is Bertilak's wife.

87 *Morgan le Fay . . . Morgan the Goddess*: Morgan was the daughter of Arthur's mother by her first husband, Gorlois, Duke of Tintagel; Arthur was her son by her second husband, Uther Pendragon. Morgan is therefore the half-sister of Arthur and the full sister of Gawain's mother. Merlin's teaching her magic is found in some French romances (Sir Thomas Malory describes her as having learned her 'nigromancie' in a nunnery). There are no authoritative forms of the legends about Morgan, however, only different versions. She frequently figures as the enemy of Arthur and the Round Table, and, in the French prose *Lancelot*, of Guinevere in particular; but her plot to frighten the queen to death is such a failure as not to register with the reader even as a possibility in the first scene at Camelot. Morgan is not called 'goddess' elsewhere in English; it has been proposed that she is a form of an early Irish goddess, the Morrigan, but there is little supporting evidence.

88 *Turned to wherever he would*: in the last sight given of Bertilak, he is still green, and not necessarily returning to his castle. Just at the moment when the poet appears to have given a full explanation of him, in which the Green Knight is merely the lord turned green, the text reopens the whole question.

tied under his left arm: worn like this, the girdle forms the heraldic device of a bend, a diagonal band running from the top right to lower left (from the point of view of the bearer, not the onlooker). The poet puns on *bend* and *band* at the start of the next stanza. One of the few secular orders of chivalry to precede Edward III's founding of the Order of the Garter was the Castilian Order of the Sash ('de la Banda'), the distinguishing mark of which was a sash worn in this manner (Richard Barber. *The Knight and Chivalry* (rev. edn., Woodbridge, 1995), 340).

89 *Laughing loudly*: the court had wept when Gawain set out, so laughter on his return is a proper response to his homecoming. It need not imply mockery or superficiality, though the contrast with Gawain's extreme (and perhaps excessive) self-abasement is marked.

lords and ladies . . . honoured evermore: the poet is describing the creation of an order of knighthood comparable to the Order of the Garter, instituted by Edward III in *c*.1348 (and see the last note below). In contrast to the Round Table, ladies were admitted to the Order of the Garter, as they are to the order of the green girdle. The relevance to contemporary orders of knighthood was also recognized by the redactor of *The Green Knight*, a late verse rewriting of the story, in which the adventures of Gawain become a foundation legend for the wearing of a white lace by knights created according to the ceremonial of the Order of the Bath (text ed. Thomas Hahn, *Sir Gawain: Eleven Romances and Tales* (Kalamazoo, Mich., 1995)).

I pray . . . Amen: a prayer for blessing is a conventional way of closing a story, but the particular formula may have been carefully chosen: the contrast of the crown of thorns worn by Christ at the Crucifixion and the 'joy' of Heaven recalls the 'delight and horror' of the opening stanza, just as the poem returns for its closure to the founding of Britain by Brutus and the fall of Troy.

Honi soyt qui mal pense: the motto of the Order of the Garter, 'Shamed be the one who thinks evil'. The words are appropriate both for the circumstances of the founding of the 'order of the green girdle', and for the kind of multiple judgements offered at the end of the poem: shame and honour are in the mind of the beholder, whether of Gawain in his self-abasement at his fall from perfection, of Bertilak in his condemnation of Gawain's fault and delight in his degree of success, or of the members of the court who demonstrate their own honourableness through their recognition of Gawain's achievement. The presence of the motto could also indicate some connection between a historical knight of the Garter and the composition of the poem, or—perhaps more likely, since the motto is written in a different hand from the rest of the text—the commissioning or ownership of this particular volume. Sir John Stanley was one of the few Garter knights from the appropriate dialect area; he was not incorporated into the Order until some years after the likely dates of the composition and copying of the poem (see Introduction, p. xvi), but the indication that the motto is a later addition would fit with that.

	Classical Literary Criticism
	Greek Lyric Poetry
ARISTOTLE	The Nicomachean Ethics
	Physics
	Politics
CAESAR	The Civil War
	The Gallic War
CATULLUS	The Poems of Catullus
EURIPIDES	Medea, Hippolytus, Electra, and Helen
HERODOTUS	The Histories
HOMER	The Iliad
	The Odyssey
HORACE	The Complete Odes and Epodes
JUVENAL	The Satires
MARCUS AURELIUS	The Meditations
OVID	The Love Poems
	Metamorphoses
	Sorrows of an Exile
PETRONIUS	The Satyricon
PLATO	Defence of Socrates, Euthyphro, and Crito
	Republic
PLAUTUS	Four Comedies
SOPHOCLES	Antigone, Oedipus the King, and Electra
VIRGIL	The Aeneid
	The Eclogues and Georgics

The Oxford World's Classics Website

www.worldsclassics.co.uk

- Information about new titles
- Explore the full range of Oxford World's Classics
- Links to other literary sites and the main OUP webpage
- Imaginative competitions, with bookish prizes
- Peruse *Compass*, the Oxford World's Classics magazine
- Articles by editors
- Extracts from Introductions
- A forum for discussion and feedback on the series
- Special information for teachers and lecturers

www.worldsclassics.co.uk

American Literature

British and Irish Literature

Children's Literature

Classics and Ancient Literature

Colonial Literature

Eastern Literature

European Literature

History

Medieval Literature

Oxford English Drama

Poetry

Philosophy

Politics

Religion

The Oxford Shakespeare

A complete list of Oxford Paperbacks, including Oxford World's Classics, OPUS, Past Masters, Oxford Authors, Oxford Shakespeare, Oxford Drama, and Oxford Paperback Reference, is available in the UK from the Academic Division Publicity Department, Oxford University Press, Great Clarendon Street, Oxford OX2 6DP.

In the USA, complete lists are available from the Paperbacks Marketing Manager, Oxford University Press, 198 Madison Avenue, New York, NY 10016.

Oxford Paperbacks are available from all good bookshops. In case of difficulty, customers in the UK can order direct from Oxford University Press Bookshop, Freepost, 116 High Street, Oxford OX1 4BR, enclosing full payment. Please add 10 per cent of published price for postage and packing.